THE
WARRIOR'S
SAVIOR

In the Best of Times and the Worst of Times

Robert Lancaster

Fulton Books
Meadville, PA

Published by Fulton Books 2024

ISBN 979-8-89221-283-0 (paperback)
ISBN 979-8-89221-284-7 (digital)

Printed in the United States of America

Having the opportunity to fly with and learn from Chief Warrant Officers Ron Stephens and Richard Hutchinson were truly eye-opening experiences. Only a warrant officer could appreciate their abilities. I wish them the best. Thank you, Ron and Rich, the best helicopter pilots in the world. And *Professor Julie Andrade*, the professor who first planted the seed of the joy of writing.

I would say this Bud's for y'all, but we don't drink Bud anymore! Be safe.

CONTENTS

PROLOGUE

The director eluded very clearly, "We cannot afford to have any of this information leaked before our mission has been completed."

He then asked, "Do we have an understanding? I would like to hear each one of you say yes or express your desire to secede from this mission now."

He said, "DeLisa?"

She said, "Yes."

"Ron?"

He said, "Yes."

"Rob?"

I said, "Yes."

The director went on to say, "This could get really hairy real fast, but you have plenty of time to prepare and practice. Ron, I expect you to oversee this mission in its entirety. You are the mission commander."

Continuing his briefing, the director stated, "DeLisa, I have reserved a range just for you and your team for the next two weeks. Your team will be the only people on the range, so whatever scenarios and conditions you need or want, let Ron know, and we will support him in supplying those needs."

He went on to say, "Ron, you will be the mission commander and intelligence liaison for this tasking and have full authority to terminate the mission if detection is imminent."

In acknowledging my responsibilities, he stated, "Rob, you're being assigned as the air mission commander. You're going to be the lead aircraft for a three-ship mission. You're inserting two six-man teams, waiting for their mission completion, and then extracting them upon their return to your location. The only people on your aircraft going to the LZ will be three snipers for team overwatch protection and then the package for extraction. I will allow you to choose your own flight crews with Ron's approval or suggestions. This will be a night-vision-goggle mission, so train appropriately. You're looking at about a ninety-kilometer distance to your LZ from your insertion point on the border."

Getting more in depth, he said, "Now, DeLisa, coming with Scott are two people you know pretty well, shooter's David J. and Chuck C. You will be in charge of the overwatch team. Where and how you set up will be determined by you. Your responsibility is to provide cover for the teams during their extraction of the package and to ensure our package gets to the LZ."

Looking at DeLisa, I was floored. Her duties with the over-watch team meant she was a shooter. She wouldn't look at me; she just kept looking down.

CHAPTER 1

Warrior's Savior Refresher

After coming back to the US and pushing the Iran-Contra debacle behind me, my thoughts were concentrated on the one aspect of my life that meant everything. Having the most astonishing surprise while in Honduras and coming to the realization that the woman of my dreams was forever lost, then discovering her again in the fashion that I did and in a faraway land were like guardian angels protecting me and ensuring my happiness in life would never disappear.

If you remember in the first book of the series, *The Warrior's Savior*, after high school, the love of my life, DeLisa, and I had been separated for almost twelve years before running into each other again in Honduras. The traumatic occurrence of us running into each other was the most shock and awe event I experienced. To this day, my true belief of us finding each other had to have been fate. Flying a gunshot victim from the Contras back to our hospital with our medevac helicopter slightly shot up and my crew chief grazed by small-arms fire in the right shoulder, our situation became even more dire when flying to the only airfield available. Discovering the airfield had been covered by a solid cloud bank and not having enough fuel to take the patient anywhere else, we had no choice but to ask the air traffic controllers for a ground control approach (GCA), precision approach. Having practiced this approach with the GCA controllers on numerous occasions, I was familiar but very uncomfortable with

1

it. With the cloud bank almost to the ground, I talked to the controller on the radio and requested a GCA approach.

The controller asked, "Is this Hoot?"

I replied, stating, "Yes, this is Hoot," which was my call sign, and all the controllers were aware of the name "Hoot."

The controller said, "Stand by."

Suddenly, a female controller came on the radio and said, "It's good to hear your voice, Hoot."

I recognized that she was the one I had trained with so many times.

As she read me the weather on the airfield, the weather was below the required minimums for the approach. We had practiced taking the aircraft to the ground on every practice approach with her. Knowing it was going to be her talking me down gave me confidence that she would be the perfect controller in talking us down safely to the runway.

As she talked us down, we reached what was known as decision height, which meant we had to decide to go around or, if we could see certain lights, we could continue the approach. Well, at two hundred feet, we could not see lights or anything else, but we had no choice but to continue the approach to the ground.

As she said, "Decision height, say intentions."

I said "continue approach" and told Chip, my copilot, to call out the altitude in twenty-feet intervals.

The controller said, "On course, on glide path."

The copilot said, "160 feet, 140 feet."

The controller said, "On course, on glide path."

Backing my airspeed off to forty knots and correcting my descent rate to less than three hundred feet per minute, I began "riding the shutter" the rest of the way down.

The copilot said, "One hundred feet, eighty feet, I have the *runway. I have the controls.*"

Surrendering the controls to Chip, I looked up, and the runway centerline was right below us. Getting on the radio, I stated, "Runway insight, request frequency change to ground."

She said, "Roger, Hoot. Change to frequency 128.30 to tower. They are taking over for ground. Frequency change approved, and have a good night."

After hovering into the parking area, I told Chip to maintain communications with tower and to wait for the ambulance. I needed to talk to the GCA controller again.

He said, "Okay, I have the controls and the radio."

After switching the frequency to GCA, I said, "GCA, this is Dustoff 367."

She said, "Dustoff 367, this is GCA, go ahead."

Stating in an exhaustively humbling voice, I said, "Just wanted to thank you for a great approach. You saved lives today, not to speak of my bacon, and I just wanted to thank you so much."

She said, "You're the one who flew the approach. That was a great job, Hoot!"

I said, "Thanks, but without you, I would not have made it down. By the way, as thanks, can I buy you breakfast in the morning at our wonderfully exquisite Army dining facility?"

After hearing her laugh over the radio, she said, "I will be at the bottom of the entrance stairs at eight a.m. Is that good for you?"

I said, "I would be honored."

Normally, on a temporary assignment and being assigned to a location for such a short period of time, the pilots do not have an opportunity to meet the air traffic controllers. Not knowing who this controller was developed an anxiety and made me so nervous for some reason. There was something about her voice that gave me a comforting emotion I had not felt in a long time.

When it came time to go to breakfast, I took Scotty, my crew chief, with me for support. Scotty had seen her before and knew who she was, but he did not know we knew each other. He also stated that she was a stunningly gorgeous woman.

I thought to myself, *Scotty is accustomed in dating anything that could breathe, walk, or dance that wore a skirt, so for him to say she is good-looking was questionable, at best.*

As we turned the corner from around the building, she was facing away from us, reading something, so she did not hear us com-

3

ing up behind her. Looking at her from the back, Scott was right; she did look exquisite. Remembering the instant she turned around due to her sensing someone was behind her and perceiving her total disbelief in recognizing that it was me was a moment in time I will never forget.

Observing her eyes beginning to water, I heard the quiver of her voice when she asked, "Rob?"

My unbelievable astonishment and shock—almost hurling me backward, flabbergasted by the woman of my dreams whom, at the time, I had come to believe I would never see again—reenergized those awkward moments in high school when I could not speak, breathe, or function normally around her. Scotty could not believe his eyes. He held my arm because he thought I was going to hit the ground. Leaning on Scotty and regaining my balance, I walked closer to her; seeing tears trekking down her face, I placed my right hand gently on her cheek.

She lost it, throwing her arms around my shoulders.

Feeling her breath on my neck and then knowing she was real and discovering the wetness of her tears on the bottom side of my chin, it finally hit me like a .50 caliber machine gun taking me out: this was DeLisa, the one and only true love of my life.

Suddenly, I could hear Scott say, "It's obvious you two have a past, and before I join you guys in a crying orgy, I am going in to eat some breakfast. Would you two like me to reserve a table or are you guys just going to go get a hotel room?"

We both looked at Scott and said, "Just go away!"

We never made it to breakfast; we just talked and talked. It was like we were making love with our words, touching and kissing each other, and then reality hit when she had four minutes before her shift started.

We decided that she would come to the medevac operations building after she got off her shift.

Honestly, that day was the longest day of my life, waiting for her to complete her shift. The entire day waiting for her felt like a dream or fantasy that was not real.

Dosing off in the afternoon heat in the hammock on the porch, the shock of seeing DeLisa, touching her, talking to her, and kissing her, I thought, *This meeting has to be a dream.* I have a memory of being rudely awakened and being startled. Opening my eyes, DeLisa was looking down at me, and all the guys around were laughing. I thought I had said something in my sleep, but apparently, I didn't. *Thank you, Lord!*

The next three and a half months were filled with some of the most sensuous times of my life, and without question, DeLisa felt the same way.

After Honduras, we both agreed to meet up at Fort Rucker, Alabama, where I had to attend instructor pilot school and she had to attend advanced NCO school for air traffic controllers. Both schools were at Fort Rucker, and we decided to live together while we were there.

While at Fort Rucker, asking DeLisa to marry me materialized, and she seemed to be the happiest woman I had ever known. After saying yes, we both had to go back to our perspective bases, me to Fort Stewart, Georgia, and her to Fort Hood, Texas.

CHAPTER 2

Dealing with the Past

Upon her return to Fort Hood, Texas, she was notified that she was going to receive orders transferring her to Ansbach, Germany. When she told me about her transfer, I talked to my assignments officer at Fort Stewart. The closest assignment to her available for me would be a flying position in the 701st Military Intelligence Group out of Augsburg, Germany. It was about an hour-drive away from Ansbach. We decided to put off marriage until we were in Germany, seeing that our assignments had already been executed by the Army.

I was surprised at being assigned to a position that was normally reserved for senior warrant officers. The unit had only six pilots and three aircraft. All the warrant officers were CW4s (chief warrant officer 4), and one was a CW3 on the promotion list to CW4. The unit had one captain who was our detachment commander, and he was one of the six pilots. Our aviation detachment supported intelligence operators from the most southern tip of what is now called Czechia all the way to the northern border of Germany above Hamburg. We supported numerous intelligence operations and supported the many listening posts along the entire border. Being the only pilots in an entire brigade proved to be a very prestigious position. I cannot tell you how many times an intelligence person approached me, asking about being a pilot.

Before I could start flying missions for the unit, my security clearance had to be upgraded from secret to a secret-crypto due to the people and equipment we flew. During the upgrade, a background investigation had to be performed and completed prior to me flying any intelligence missions.

Walking into the office at the airfield one morning, our dispatcher said, "Sir, the commander wanted to see you as soon as you arrived."

I said "Thanks, I'll go right now," thinking my clearance investigation had been completed.

Knocking on the door and hearing the commander say "enter," I entered his office, and to my surprise, there were two investigators from the US Army CID (Criminal Investigative Division) with my commander. They wanted to talk to me in depth about my tour in Honduras with Eugene "Chip" Tatum.

One of them looked at me and asked, "Tell me about Chip Tatum."

At that point, I knew where this was going. Because of my affiliation in working with Chip Tatum (a CIA operative), they were going to give me a difficult time of approving my clearance or disapprove it all together. They were in for a stark awakening no one else had ever been exposed to.

Before Chip actually infiltrated my medevac unit at Fort Stewart, I had been contacted and, you might say, recruited to perform surveillance on Chip Tatum, my pilot in command. I would be working directly for CIA Director C. and NSA M. because they didn't want any American military members hurt, caught up in, or sacrificed due to operations of the Iran-Contra enterprise. Chip never knew that I was reporting to Director C. after every completed mission. The direction I was given by the director was basically, if any American troops or flight crew members were being put in unnecessary danger by intelligence or Contra members dealing with the transportation of drugs, I was to report to him at the earliest possible moment. Under all cost, I was never to reveal my reporting to the director to anyone except the national security advisor, and I didn't. Additionally, if anything was ever exposed that I thought would be detrimental to my career, I was to give Director C. or the Advisor M. a call at the number he had provided.

Looking at my commander, I said, "Sir, I apologize, but I am going to have to ask you to leave the room. The questions these investigators are asking are going to have to be treated with the highest security. To answer these questions, I am under orders to initiate a telephone call and have them ask any questions they may have to the individual I call, which is classified. I am under orders to perform this procedure."

My commander said, "Rob, no problem." Then my commander, turning and looking at the investigators, said with extreme clarity, "You can use my phone, fellows, and I will only say this once. You guys better not be on a witch hunt! Do you understand?"

One of the investigators said, "Yes, sir, we just need clarification on some issues," *which is code for: I am going to try and catch you in something to prevent you from getting any kind of clearance.*

Sitting at my commander's desk, I dialed the number the director had given me, and to my surprise, the CIA director's office answered.

I stated, "Medevac, Lancaster, 1133."

Almost immediately, the National Security Advisor M. answered the phone, and we went secure.

"Mr. Lancaster," he said, "what can I do for you today?"

I said, "Sir, in my new position, it is required for me to get an upgraded security clearance. During the background investigation, two CID investigators are in my commander's office in front of me asking questions about Eugene 'Chip' Tatum and my involvement with him while in Honduras. I need your assistance in the answers. Can I put you on speaker?"

The advisor said, "Yes, by all means, put me on."

As I put everyone on speaker, one of the CID investigators started to speak. "Mr. Advisor, we are here to ascertain what role Mr. Lancaster performed while being assigned with Mr. Chip Tatum in Honduras and—"

Interrupting the agent very forcibly, the advisor stated in no uncertain terms, "Mr. Investigator, ascertain this. Mr. Lancaster was working for the CIA director and myself *directly*, reporting to me, and had *no involvement* with Mr. Tatum's actions. Mr. Lancaster was a medical evacuation pilot and probably the best I've ever had the honor of knowing. Now, unless you can prove presidential authority, you will close any and all investigations against Mr. Lancaster and approve his clearance as requested and with an indisputable, flawless record. Is that clear?"

Then the advisor continued to probe the CID agents by saying, "By the way, who instructed you to investigate Mr. Lancaster? And do not mess with me or it will be your career, and I mean before you even leave the building you are sitting in!"

As the wheels were turning in the investigators' head, one of them said, "Sir, the request came from the office of our commander at Third Army. Beyond that, it is above my pay grade, and I do not know."

The national security advisor said, "Gentlemen, give Mr. Lancaster a copy of your orders to investigate him. Mr. Lancaster, fax those orders to me immediately. Now do you fellows have any further questions?"

The investigators said, "No, sir. All is clear. Thank you, sir."

After they left, my commander came back in and said, "I know you cannot discuss your situation with Mr. Chip Tatum, but just to let you know, I have been read in and briefed on these guys trying to find a reason to delay or find reason to terminate your clearance. I also know about your flying abilities and how well you performed in the 'bush' of Honduras. Not many Army aviators earn the Joint Service Meritorious Medal. That is usually reserved for the big guys who command units of several different types of military units or countries during an operation. Congratulations, I am going to assume everything went well on the telephone call, and we can start planning to put you to work soon."

Responding confidently to the commander, I said, "Yes, sir, I believe the issues of Honduras are behind me now, and personally, I am ready to get back in the air. I do have to fax something the CID gave me, though. I will do that now."

The commander yelled out to CW4 Ron S., our standardization instructor pilot. Ron came in, and the commander asked Ron to get me up as soon as possible for duty. Ron was, without question, the best pilot I have ever flown with. I thought Hutch was the greatest, but I was mistaken. Demonstrating all the maneuvers to Ron to the best of my ability, he was unexpectedly pleased. He considered my combat tactics and emergency procedures to be some of the best. He assigned me to fly with the commander as a combat crew. In Ron's opinion, I had enough "tact" to be the commander's pilot in command in an assigned combat crew. It is a very difficult position to be in. Being a pilot in command and having your commanding officer as your copilot can be touchy at times, to say the least.

As Ron assigned the commander and me together, I asked Ron, "Were you and the commander together as a combat crew before me?"

Ron looked at me and smiled and said, "Yep. You are the only other school-trained instructor pilot here besides me, and I need a break from the brass. Plus I'm your immediate boss, and 'shit rolls downhill!'"

I thought, *Wow! Among any other unit in the Army, I, the unit instructor pilot, will be the one calling the shots on the makeup of combat crew assignments. Discovering that me, the new unit instructor pilot, the one who has the ability to recommend an aviator to have additional training or to be grounded because of a flight deficiency, is having to fly with, most likely, the worst pilot in the unit, the commander.*

I looked at Ron and said, "What did I do to you to deserve this?"

Ron laughed and said, "Nothing, brother, I just needed a break, and don't worry, this aviation unit has not been in combat in a very long time."

I said, "That's good to hear."

Ron was a straight shooter and had some of the best political skills ever witnessed. When it came to "tact" and "playing politics," Ron and another CW3 in our unit were the quickest men on their feet I had ever witnessed thus far in the Army. No one besides the last commander assigned to our detachment could even come close to Ron. I believe our commander would truly agree with my assessment.

10

CHAPTER 3

DeLisa's Real Secret

Flying with the commander was kind of a pain in the rear, but after a few flights, we began to know each other's expected responsibilities in the cockpit, and it was working out fairly well.

Finding an apartment about thirty minutes away from the airfield and about half way to Ansbach, where DeLisa was stationed, ended up to be a perfect out-of-the-way place for DeLisa and I to set up house. We found a place in the countryside, and she seemed to be as happy as "pig in you know what!" At least, there was no reason for me to think otherwise. DeLisa was always smiling, happy, wanting to see all the shops in the little towns, and exhibiting more love for me than any man could have ever asked for in a woman.

After flying several missions to the border in support of our intelligence sites, this job seemed to be old hat and never seemed to have any surprises like my medevac days.

After about six months, something in DeLisa's personality was changing. Slowly, but changing. I found myself thinking about her changes; I started to pay close attention to her actions. She was becoming very deep in her thoughts, sometime seeming to be clandestine and secretive about normal day-to-day family issues.

Beginning to be anxious, on our next three-day weekend off from work, I planned an outing to the mountains and booked us a room in a bed-and-breakfast outside of a little town in Austria called

Linz. Being near the highest peak in the Austrian mountains, the countryside was beautiful.

On our last day, we decided to have a picnic overlooking a lake we could see outside our bedroom at the B and B. As we packed our lunch, I was able to acquire a bottle of wine from the B and B owner and a blanket to lay out on.

Arriving at the perfect scenic spot, we threw the blanket out and began enjoying a great glass of wine. Looking into her eyes, something I'd never seen before made me uncomfortable. Turning her head away from me, she tried concealing whatever she wanted to say; I could not let it pass. The probing of her thoughts seemed to be the right thing to do.

I said in a soft voice, "Dee, talk to me. What's going on?"

Looking at me with those green, piercing eyes that had stabbed my heart so many times, I was suddenly trying to be masked. By her looking down and turning her head, my heart dropped like a rock. It felt like falling out of the air in a steep dive with your stomach in your throat and not being able to say a word. I reached out and took her hand; suddenly, she pulled back, stood up, and walked a few steps away and leaned against a tree. I reached for her arm, gently turned her around, and saw her tears traversing downward on her cheeks as her lips commenced a slight quiver as they always did when she was deeply emotional. She continued looking at the ground to avoid looking into my eyes.

Suddenly looking up and staring dead into my soul with those green eyes I was so accustomed in seeing, she stated, "*Rob, I have lied to you.*"

Not knowing what she was talking about and thinking the absolute worst scenario, it felt like someone had just kicked me in my midsection. The hurt was so bad; placing my hands on my knees was all I could do to not fall to my knees. Looking up at her and holding her arm with one of my hands, I could see her shocked look at my reaction.

Suddenly, she said, "*No, no, I love you more than anything in the world. I have not been unfaithful.*"

As she said those words, feeling her genuine empathy was so comforting, and seeing the depth of her concern, I said, "What is going on then? You have been in your own little world for a few weeks now, and I have been walking on eggshells, trying to figure out where your mind is at. Just talk to me. You know I am yours and always will be."

Taking my hand and leading me back to the blanket, she said, "What I am about to tell you is classified, and you cannot disclose this to anyone. Rob, I'm not kidding. This is some serious information, and if it gets out, it can cause some potentially disastrous consequences. Do you understand?"

I said, "Yes, and if it is that important, before you go on, lay back and let me do something, no questions asked."

With a puzzled look on her face, she said, "Okay."

I took my little handheld radio out of my pocket, turned it on, and turned the volume to its full high position. Thinking to myself about everything that had happened with the CID, I knew someone had started asking questions about Honduras, and if it was those two investigators, all hell was going to break loose. Listening for the static on my little radio, I ran it all over her body, seeing if I could get any static from a bug. Bigger than life, as my radio got close to her right sneaker, lots of static commenced on my radio. As Dee started to say something, I placed my finger to her lips. She ceased and was looking at me in disbelief. I pulled a small portable listening/transmitter device off her right sneaker.

Changing my radio to a strong music station and turning the volume up to the loudest it could be, I quickly moved the speaker of the radio to the front of the bug. I observed two men across the field in the distance jerking their headsets off, quickly gathering their affects and departing the area as quickly as they could.

DeLisa looked at me with a look of total confusion and said, "Rob, what are you involved in?"

I said, "I am not involved with anything anymore. The CIA is trying to locate Chip Tatum, and they are using any and all possible resources to do just that. Do you remember Chip from Honduras?"

She said, "Yes. Now I need to tell you what I was going to tell you earlier. I knew you were in Honduras before we ran into each other. I was approached by the CIA while I was in basic training because of my degree in political science and the current job I have. They recruited me for the CIA in support of monitoring the drug traffic being transported to the US from Honduras via air transportation. I would call and give them the aircraft tail number, flight plan, and where it was going when it departed from Honduras. Now here is the kicker. The only aircraft I was to report on leaving Honduras was the aircraft you guys in medevac met up with and subsequently flew to the US."

I told her, "Hold that thought!" I was getting angry.

I called the number I had been given, and the director's office answered again just as before.

I said, "Lancaster, medevac, 1133."

DeLisa's jaw dropped open. She knew at that point that I was also working with the "company." Again, the advisor answered and stated, "Mr. Lancaster, I thought our investigators had been taken care of?"

I said, "Yes, sir, are we secure?"

The advisor said, "Yes."

I said, "Yes, sir, I thought so too. I have since discovered they or someone has bugged my fiancé's clothing for reasons I do not know. The only thing I can think of is they, whoever they are, are trying to get to Chip through me, and sir, I haven't seen Chip since he left us in the wind in Honduras. Mr. Advisor, I have completed every task you and the director has requested, and bugging my future family has crossed the line. I am getting pretty tired of people continuing their surveillance of me and now my future family. This needs to stop, and I mean it."

Interrupting me, the advisor said, "Just settle down, give me about three days, and this will all be done with. I will find out who is pulling the strings and will definitely make it go away permanently."

I said, "Thank you, sir."

Hanging up, I noticed DeLisa, lying next to me, intently monitoring every word she could make out. Not understanding the reason for the CIA to monitor several agents working for them in the same operation did not make sense to me. I found out that the director was a man who would cover every angle possible and wanted to know every player in the game. Hell, I wouldn't be surprised if he didn't already know Chip's exact location.

Looking at DeLisa, I said, "Dee, who specifically recruited you?"

She said, "I cannot remember his name, but I can describe him." DeLisa was very good in the art of drawing a person's face, and her memory was spot-on.

Then DeLisa asked, "Who were you talking to on the telephone? I need to know because the person I reported to on occasion was in the JTF-Bravo Operations in Honduras."

I told DeLisa, "My telephone call was to the national security advisor." Then I told her the reason for associating with the CIA and NSA was to ensure the safety of our military members from the CIA personnel conducting drug operations. I knew all the players in the operations in Honduras; there were an Army major, a Marine major, and the Army LT who called down all the mission requests to us for medevac. The Marine major was the only "part-time" operations officer we had. I showed DeLisa a picture of him, and she confirmed he was the one who had recruited her. That Marine major also happened to be Chip Tatum's handler.

After determining that Chip's handler was the same person who recruited DeLisa, there was a certain amount of paranoia born within me concerning DeLisa's' welfare.

As DeLisa and I were driving back to our apartment at Graben, you could see and feel her concern of being involved in these operations. She was not comfortable at all. Her continuous observation of the traffic behind us or passing us was unsettling.

Pulling off the autobahn to a rest area that had a restaurant, turning the car off, and looking at her, I said, "We are going to be okay. Have you been contacted by anyone since you have been here in Germany?"

She said, "No, there has been no contact at all, and that has been at least seven months now."

Entering the restaurant and sitting across the table from her, I could see the fear in her eyes. She didn't like the idea of being involved with the CIA, NSA, or any other agency that had the ability to terminate people's lives or their livelihood.

Taking her hand in mine and gently kissing the back of it, I said, "Don't worry, if the CIA operators do not want to play by the rules, the director will not allow something to happen to us."

She laughed, looked at me with those piercing, green eyes I was so accustomed to seeing, and said, "We missed so much time together. All I ever wanted to do from the very first day you kissed me in the hallway at school was to be with you. I didn't want to be involved with all this cloak-and-dagger stuff."

Looking at her, I asked, "Are you sure about that? What about your career in air traffic control?"

She looked at me and said, "I can work in a tower anywhere in the US when we get back to the states. I have my credentials. My reenlistment is coming up in two months, and I need to make my mind up if I'm going to stay in the Army or get out. I need to tell you more too. There is still more that you need to know about my involvement with the CIA."

Squeezing her hand gently, I said, "If you don't care for what you're doing and would prefer to get out of the Army, I will support your decision 100 percent. Do you think it's time to set a wedding date and you just go ahead and get out of the Army in two months? We could move from here and find something closer to Augsburg."

DeLisa's expressions transitioned from a worried look to a happy face again through and through. I could see it in her eyes; her desire for finalizing our marriage would provide her with the fulfillment she has been craving to experience in our relationship.

After making the suggestion, the thought of her becoming my wife and her being happy about it down to her bones brought up feelings in me that have never surfaced before. Because of her display of joy and happiness, the emotions I felt for DeLisa were suddenly becoming difficult to control. Realizing that my dream of her becoming my wife was going to be a real occurrence and not just a dream was almost overwhelming.

DeLisa saw my happiness just oozing out of my eyes, and she could feel my emotions in my hand. We were two of the happiest people in the world or at least in this particular restaurant at this particular time.

After eating and enjoying each other's company, we jumped into the car and continued on our way home.

On the way home, I did remember that she wanted to tell me something more about herself, but I thought, *What else can she say that would blow my mind? Better to let sleeping dogs lie.*

Boy, was I in for a rude awakening.

CHAPTER 4

Who's Pulling the Strings?

As we walked up to the apartment front door after we arrived, she was holding on to my arm so tightly the thought of losing my arm due to the lack of circulation seemed to be a genuine concern.

Placing the key into the door and noticing the door was unlocked, I told her to stand back on one side of the door. She had a shocked look on her face.

She said, "Rob, what is it?"

I said, "Do you remember locking the door?"

Without question, she said, "Yes, I distinctly remember checking it before we left."

Pushing the door open with my toe, seeing our apartment totally trashed was unsettling to say the least. DeLisa was so scared that she was shaking. I knew there was most likely no one there. I did not know who these people were and what they were looking for, but it didn't look like they found it. I called my commander immediately and informed him of my situation and asked if DeLisa and I could talk to him the next morning.

He said yes, and I should consider getting a room at the guest house on base in Augsburg for at least the night, and he would be in his office and see me in the morning. "Also bring DeLisa in with you in the morning. We may need to get her commander involved as well."

I agreed, and so did she.

That night, we went to the guest house on the base, and they had received a call from my commander about our needs for the night.

After settling into our room, she held me like no person had ever held me before. She was scared, and after I learned a little about the person she had to report to in Honduras, I was not feeling confident either.

Knowing there was someone out there surveilling us and trying to find Chip Tatum, it seemed evident that none of these events were making any sense. If this was all about finding Chip Tatum, the CIA and NSA had plenty of assets to find him. They didn't need to get to him through us. They had to have known by now that neither of us has been in contact with him for almost a year now.

On the way to the commanders office, we stopped to get a cup of hot coffee. Both of us were beat and bordering on exhaustion. We tossed and turned almost all night, so the coffee was a great pick-me-up for both of us.

As DeLisa and I walked into my detachment operations office, Ron, my operations officer, was waiting for us to escort us to the commander.

Knocking on his door, I expected to report to my commanding officer, but I didn't hear him say "enter" as he usually does.

Looking at Ron, he also looked puzzled. Ron said, "Let me check to see if he is busy or on the phone." He pushed the door open slightly and stuck his head in.

All I heard from Ron was, "Oh my god!"

Ron quickly closed the door, looked at me, and said, "Go get Sergeant Jacobs and hurry."

Running to operations and seeing the sergeant on the phone, I interrupted him, saying, "Ron needs you outside the commander's door *now*!"

We both ran back down the hallway toward the commander's door. Ron was not there, and neither was DeLisa. In fact, they both disappeared in just the few seconds that I was away getting the sergeant.

Sgt. Jacobs opened the commander's door, and I looked in as well.

As we stepped into his office, the commander was in his chair behind his desk, head leaned back and blood spattered all over the back of his chair. The blood spatter continued all over the wall behind him.

Sgt. Jacobs went to grab the commander, and I said, "*Wait*, do not touch anything! Bring me a 9mm."

Looking at me oddly, he said, "What do you want the 9mm for?"

I said, "I am going to secure the scene because I don't know who is behind this."

I began thinking of what happened to DeLisa and Ron.

I asked Jacobs, "Do you know what kind of vehicle Ron is driving?"

He said, "Yeah, he's in his BMW."

Looking at Jacobs, I said, "Is his Beemer still in the parking lot?"

Sgt. Jacobs looked out the window and said, "Yes, there it is. Sir, what is going on?"

I said, "Sergeant, go to the armory and get yourself and me a 9mm now, and I'll fill you in when you get back. Make sure you secure the armory after you get the two 9mm's."

While he was gone, I made a call to the director. When someone picked up, I stated, "Medevac, Lancaster, 1133."

The advisor answered and said, "Mr. Lancaster, I have not finished trying to determine who's behind the surveillance of you and your fiancé yet."

Interrupting him, I said, "I believe my fiancé and our operations officer have been abducted, and I have just found my commander in his office shot in the head, and he's dead."

He said, "Does anyone else know what's happened?"

I said, "My first sergeant knows that our commander is dead, and our operations officer and DeLisa is nowhere to be found."

The advisor said, "I'm sending a team in to take care of everything. They should be there in less than two hours. Do not call anyone, no military police or Criminal Investigation Division, *absolutely no one, do you understand!* And secure that building, no one in or out."

I said, "Yes, sir."

I sat down on the floor with my back against the wall, looked at Sgt. Jacobs, and said, "Sarge, all I can tell you is that my fiancé and I had an appointment with the commander this morning to try and figure out who was surveilling us and who trashed our apartment sometime this last weekend. Both DeLisa and I were involved with CIA operations while in Honduras, and the guy I was flying with in Honduras has disappeared. No one can find him."

Sarge asked, "What kind of operations were you involved in while in Honduras?"

I explained. "We were right in the middle of the Iran-Contra affair."

He said, "Sir, you guys are in some shit. Haven't you been watching the news? People are having to testify before Congress for that operation. There could be some high-stakes consequences about to happen to you and your fiancé. But one of the good things is that if your fiancé is with Ron, she will be okay."

I looked at him and said, "Why do you say that?"

He said, "Sir, being in intelligence for the last twenty-four years, you get to know who the good guys and the bad guys are. Even if they know how to play the spy game, I can pick out the bad guys, and Ron is definitely *not* a bad guy. It might be the best thing that has happened to your fiancé to have him around her right now. Sir, Ron is one of those guys who knows everything and everybody. Do not ever underestimate Ron."

I muttered to myself, "God, I hope so."

As Sergeant Jacobs locked the building down, all I wanted to do was to find DeLisa. I walked out the rear door of the building, taking me directly into the hangar. Looking around, I found an earring on the hangar floor. It was part of a set of earrings I had given to DeLisa while in Austria. Looking at the earring, there was no blood on it, so I assumed she had dropped it on purpose to let me know she had been through here.

Knowing we had four security cameras overseeing the three aircraft and the pedestrian door in the hangar, I ran to the computer room and began searching the recording for Ron and DeLisa. On the recording, the building door opened, exposing Ron and DeLisa exiting. Ron had a handgun that looked like a 9mm just like ours. He and DeLisa were being very cautious in moving through the hangar when suddenly, five men completely surrounded them with their weapons drawn and aiming at them. You could see Ron dropping his weapon and the other men securing Ron and DeLisa's hands with ties. They were escorted out the pedestrian door of the hangar and into a black box van with no windows.

Not wanting to wait around for the NSA team to arrive, I was biting at the bit to start looking for the box van DeLisa had been forced into. Observing the commander's office, especially around and on his desk, I found a personnel file folder on me. Quickly looking through it, I came across a section that was titled "Known Associates."

As I opened it, DeLisa's name popped off the page at me. Fulfilling my curiosity, I began reading the information on her. It seemed DeLisa's file was fairly large. I said quietly to myself, "She has been CIA for years."

Suddenly hearing some commotion coming in the front door and in operations, I placed all the information about DeLisa in my pockets, secured the remainder of the file inside the desk, walked out the commander's office, and stood outside his door. No more than a minute later, three plainclothes agents started walking out the operations office toward me down the hallway.

When one of them saw me, he said, "Are you Lancaster?"

I said, "Yes."

The same guy said, "I'm Agent Jennings. Is the commander in there?"

I said, "Yes. It's *not* a pretty sight. Agent, I know you guys want to know what happened here, but we have two people who were kidnapped, and we have proof of them being abducted on our computer security cameras. One of them is my fiancé, DeLisa Lawrence, and the other is our operations officer, Ron S. We need to find that van now before these guys go crazy on one or both of them."

"Hey, hey, try to settle down. We know exactly where the van is, and our people are handling that situation as we speak. We picked the van up departing this location on satellite. We should be getting word on their situation any minute, so try to calm down. I promise you, we are all over it."

Explaining to Agent Jennings what happened and how we found my commander, Jennings explained that my commander had been under surveillance for almost a year, and the reason he was terminated had nothing to do with me or Chip Tatum.

Having a confused look on my face, he said, "DeLisa has been CIA for about six years now. I have even been on missions with her." He said, "I remember one mission distinctly. She saved my butt. At the same time, Mr. Lancaster, I know you too. You flew out and picked up one of my guys in Honduras one time when nobody else would come because of the location. In certain circles, you and DeLisa are known pretty well. Your known for different things, but both names are well-respected. Be aware that if something happens to Ron or DeLisa, there will be hell to pay."

At that very moment, the commander's telephone began to ring.

As Agent Jennings answered, he said, "Yes, sir, he is right here." He passed the telephone to me.

I said, "Hello, this is Mr. Lancaster."

"Mr. Lancaster, this is Director C. SFC Lawrence and CW4 Ron S. have been recovered, and they are in good shape. I didn't want to tell you everything was okay and act prematurely, so I kept it quiet until we knew for sure. They are being transported to your location as we speak."

I said, "Director, thank you for the call. It's a big weight off my shoulders."

The director changed the subject, suddenly going right into DeLisa, stating, "You do know DeLisa has been CIA in the past, don't you?"

Being a little confused on where this was going, I muttered, "Sir, in the past, I had suspicions something was never said or explained.

With our relationship as it is and knowing each other in so much depth and knowing the company as I do, taking a path of silence and not asking any questions seemed to be the correct direction."

I heard him laugh and say, "Rob, you and DeLisa are two of the smartest people I know when it comes to maintaining clandestine information, and I thank you both for that."

He continued to say, "Now let's get into the commander's situation. Your commander has been involved with some real shady characters. He was running a smuggling operation under the cover of an import company in Fort Lauderdale, Florida. The operation was smuggling cocaine from Syria through Hungary, Austria, and then to him in Augsburg. He would then make molds out of the powdered cocaine that looked like grandfather clocks in a clock company located in the Black Forest outside of Stuttgart. Many Americans purchased and transferred grandfather clocks out of Southern Germany to the United States every day, so seeing a sealed-up crate labeled as a grandfather clock was not uncommon for the shipping companies. They never opened the crates to examine the contents. It was one of those perfect hide in plain sight' kind of situations."

Elaborating, he said, "What triggered your commander's demise was the telephone call you made to us when the CID was in his office. There were bad guys constantly watching your commander because of his own operation, and when they saw the authorities in his office asking about your relationship with Chip, rather than ask him any questions, they just terminated him. It's a sad day when some of our troops get involved with money-making schemes that destroy them and their families just for a few dollars."

He stated, "This is all going to come out, and the CID is going to 'eat some crow,' if you know what I mean. They were so concerned in trying to seize the headlines of being the agency that subdued 'the infamous Chip Tatum' that all other incidents were pushed to the side. This operation should have been discovered and interrupted by the CID months ago, and because of their narrow focus, they missed the entire boat. Now they have also been caught illegally surveilling you and DeLisa. One of our agents was almost exposed when you identified the bug on DeLisa's shoe, then blasted the music into their ears. Our agent surveilling the CID who was surveilling you was laughing so hard he came close to exposing himself to those very agents he was observing. When I read the report, I laughed for at least an hour myself."

He went on, stating, "At that point, I knew you were aware of DeLisa being involved with the 'company,' but even at this juncture, I do not think you know how much in depth her contributions have been. Please do me a favor. When she gets back to the office, call me, and I would like to talk to both of you and Mr. Ron S. when they become available."

In a humbling voice, I said, "Yes, sir, will do, and, sir, again, thank you for looking out after DeLisa and me."

As I terminated the telephone call from the director, I began putting all the pieces together. The piece giving me the most concern was DeLisa's involvement with the company. The other piece was how Ron knew to act in trying to protect DeLisa? Was he with the company too?

Sitting in operations, I could see a black sedan pull up and stop in front of our building. What looked like a plainclothes agent exited the passenger's front seat, traversed around the rear of the vehicle, and opened the back driver's side door for DeLisa and Ron to exit the sedan.

Running to the front door, shoving it open, and slamming it into the wall helped curve my unimaginable longing for DeLisa by sprinting to her in the most direct path. She looked up and saw me running to her, and as we came together, she wrapped her arms around me so tight. Feeling her entire body shaking and hearing her distressed breathing, I sat her down on the ground so she could settle down.

Ron came walking up and said, "Is she all right?"

DeLisa interrupted me, looked up at him, and said, "Yes, I am fine now. I just want to sit out here with Rob for a few minutes to get my bearings, and Ron, thank you."

Ron, patting me on my shoulder, walked away and back into operations.

DeLisa turned to me and said, "Rob, who were those guys? No one is telling me anything!"

Gently taking her hand and hugging her with my other arm, I said, "Those guys had nothing to do with our situation in Honduras or Chip Tatum. The situation that happened here was brought on by the illegal actions of my ex-commander. In a nutshell, he was smuggling drugs into the US, and the guys he was working with didn't like the idea of him talking to the CID, so they killed him. What the smugglers didn't know was he was not talking to the CID about them. He was talking to the CID about my clearance. The people the commander was dealing with were some of the worst criminals in Germany."

After telling her that, she hugged me and said, "I want to go home and just be with you."

I told her softly, "Baby, I know, that's all I want to do too. When I couldn't find you, I had never been more worried and scared in my whole life. I also hate to tell you this, but we can't go home until we talk to the director, his orders, not mine."

She looked puzzled and worried at the same time. Being curious myself at what the director wanted to talk to us about, I got to my feet and pulled DeLisa up as well. We both walked together into the operations where Ron was sitting at his desk.

As DeLisa sat in a chair in front of the counter, I walked around and told Ron, "Brother, thank you for looking out after DeLisa. I cannot tell you how much that meant to me."

He looked at me and said, "Hey, we are both warrant officers, instructor pilots, and Texans! You can't be much more on one page than that, *Hoot*!"

Hearing him call me "Hoot" was rather special coming from him.

I told him, "By the way, the director wanted us to give him a call when you and DeLisa got back."

He looked at me and said, "I don't have his number. How in the world are we going to call him?"

"Don't worry, I have it," I said.

Looking at me with envy in his eyes, Ron said, "How do you have his number?"

I said "I'm Hoot!" and laughed.

CHAPTER 5

The Wall

Ron and DeLisa followed me into a private room, and DeLisa and Ron watched me intently calling in.

As the person answered the telephone, I said, "Lancaster, medevac, 1133."

They said "stand by," and the director came on the phone. "Mr. Lancaster, is everyone there?"

Answering him, I said, "Yes, sir, CW4 Ron S. and SFC DeLisa L. are here with me, and we are on speaker, are we secure?"

He said yes and began by saying, "Ron, how are you? It's been a long time, and, DeLisa, are you okay?"

Ron pointed at Delisa and designated her to answer and to talk first, then he stated, "Sir, we are all in good shape. Tired but all good."

He said, "People, we have a situation, and I think you're the team that can pull this off. Mikhail Gorbachev has agreed secretly, with President Reagan's support, in tearing the wall down."

We looked at one another in total astonishment. All the incidents over the past thirty years we had reacted to in halting the spread of communism in the world and, on occasion, coming close to nuclear annihilation culminated in his one sentence. It was truly like the world's weight being lifted off our shoulders.

I said, "Sir, this is unbelievable! Do you mean the Berlin Wall?"

He said, "That's the one."

Ron spoke up, saying, "Sir, what's going to be our role in this?"

The director stated, "Ron, you should be receiving a secure package via secure carrier within the hour. It explains each one of your roles in this mission. The secure carrier is someone you know, Mr. Lancaster. It's Scott C. He will be one of your crew members on this mission once his current mission of delivering the package to Mr. Ron S. is complete."

He went on to say, "If anyone wants out of this mission after they are read in by Ron, they will be transferred immediately to Fort Greely, Alaska, until the wall comes down. Is that clear? We cannot afford to have any of this information leaked before our mission has been completed."

He then asked, "Do we have an understanding? I would like to hear each one of you say yes or express your desire to secede from this mission now, and you are being recorded."

He said, "DeLisa?"

She said, "Yes."

"Ron?"

He said, "Yes."

"Rob?"

I said, "Yes."

The director went on to say, "This mission could get really hairy real fast, but you have plenty of time to prepare and practice. Ron, I expect you to oversee this mission in its entirety. You will be the mission commander. DeLisa, I have reserved a range just for you and your team for the next two weeks. Your team will be the only people on the range, so whatever scenarios and conditions you need or want, let Ron know, and we will support him in supplying those needs."

He went on to say, "Ron, you will be the mission commander and intelligence liaison for this task and have full authority to terminate the mission if detection is imminent.

"Rob, you're being assigned as the air mission commander. You're going to be lead aircraft for a three-ship mission. You're inserting two six-man teams, waiting for their mission completion, and extracting them upon their return to your location. The only people on your aircraft will be three snipers for team overwatch protection and the package for extraction. I will allow you to choose your own flight crews with Ron's approval or suggestions. This will be a night-vision-goggle mission, so train appropriately. You're looking at about a ninety-kilometer distance to your LZ from your insertion point from the border.

"Now, DeLisa, coming with Scott are two people you know pretty well, shooters David J. and Chuck C. You will be in charge of the overwatch team. Where and how you set up will be determined by you. Your responsibility is to provide cover for the teams for the extraction and to ensure our package gets onboard."

Looking at DeLisa, I was floored. Her duties with the overwatch team meant she was a shooter. She wouldn't look at me; she just kept looking down.

Then the director's voice changed to a very stern, demanding, and serious type of authority, saying, "This is not an operation that requires the assurance of everyone coming home. Rob, once the package is on board your aircraft, you are to extract immediately. No questions asked! Is that understood?"

I said, "Yes, sir."

He went on to say, "The other two aircraft have the responsibility to extract the teams and the shooters. Rob, if you have the package and you wait and something goes wrong, the entire mission will be in vain, and if that happens, your butt will be mine. Only if the shooters or some of the team members are at the helicopter and on board at takeoff will you extract them. Is this completely clear? You are not to wait for anyone. If you're running and the package is aboard, you pull pitch. I cannot emphasize this enough."

I said, "Understood, sir."

Looking at DeLisa, I knew she was CIA, but like the director stated earlier, I didn't know to what extent she was involved. Discovering in this briefing that DeLisa was a shooter, some say a sniper, and apparently a good one was, for me, devastating. Being truly speechless, after the briefing, I had to just walk outside to be alone for a while and to just contemplate the possibility of losing DeLisa on this mission.

Walking around to the rear of the building, sitting on the top of a picnic table, and reliving today's events, I realized exhaustion was creeping up on me quickly. With my mind consistently moving at what seemed to be the speed of light throughout today's events and observing today being a perfect day but at the same time an emotional one, I had become a total wreck. Again, thinking of DeLisa so deeply and knowing, when the package gets to my aircraft, I would have to make the decision to leave her if she would not be at the LZ made me feel an emptiness and sadness I haven't felt since getting separated from her when initially departing for the Army. That day, leaving her for the Army and being the loneliest day ever faced, pales in comparison to the possibility of our upcoming mission parameters.

Sitting on the picnic table, I felt her presence on my right rear side; turning my head, she said, "Rob, Ron has received the mission documents, and Scotty and my team has arrived."

As she spoke, I continued looking out across the German countryside, seeing those green fields, the Austrian mountains visible in the distance, and couldn't, at that moment, look at her with the thought of intentionally leaving her somewhere that she might have to escape and evade just to get home. The thought of her getting caught was unthinkable.

She placed her left hand on the back of my neck and moved in front of me, blocking my view of the mountains. Slowly looking up and gazing into her laser-green eyes, she could see I was really concerned about this mission, and she said so softly, "Don't worry, I will be okay. I have done this before, and no one is better at this job."

She leaned down, now with both her hands on each side of my face, and gave me the most sensuous kiss ever experienced. As she hugged me, I could hear someone coming around the corner of the building. It was Scotty.

I said, "Oh my gosh! Scotty, is that really you?"

He said as he laughed, "Yes, sir, they had to call the best to take care of the best. I see there is no changes with you two!" Then he said, "Mr. Ron S. wants us inside for the mission brief."

I looked at DeLisa and said, "It's time. Let's go."

As we all sat in the briefing room, we all introduced ourselves to one another.

One of the shooter's looked at me and said, "So you're the one. Sir, it's an honor to work with you. You extracted a member of my team from a medical facility in El Salvador in the mid-eighties, and he is alive today because of you. Sir, thank you, he was my son. The thought of losing him was a devastating thought for me, but you came through for both of us. It's an honor to know you're on this mission."

The introductions were behind us, and everyone knew I had orders that once the package was on board my aircraft, I was to leave immediately, no matter what. The package was a Soviet courier going to the White House with a message for President Reagan in alerting the administration of the timing for the Berlin Wall to come down. Many high-level politicians within the USSR did not want this event to become reality, and if they would have known the timing of the event, it would have given them the opportunity to plan some kind of reprisal.

All the shooters, including DeLisa, were sergeant first class (E-7s) and very competent at their profession.

The briefing finally concluded with Ron and me meeting tomorrow morning for the selection of two flight crews and a copilot for me. He had a list drawn up already, so tomorrow, the intent was to interview them all and make selections.

DeLisa and the other two shooters were departing for the range at approximately 0500 hours and would depart the range at 1600 hours, returning home.

DeLisa went to the ladies' room, which gave me the opportunity to talk to Dave, the guy who thanked me for extracting his son out of El Salvador. Explaining that DeLisa was my fiancé, I said to him, "I know you guys watch over one another while in the bush. If you would do me a personal favor, though, please have DeLisa's back. Sergeant, I don't know what I would do if something happened to her. Just asking you, man to man."

He said as he placed his hand on my right shoulder, "Sir, if you wanted me to carry her out on my back, I would do it. Now let me tell you something about SFC DeLisa Lawrence. She and I took out almost an entire OPFOR company from a mile away in an overwatch operation with the DEA in Colombia. She can hold her own. Personally, sir, I'm glad she is with me and Chuck. She is the best shooter I have ever worked with. If we have to E & E, we will be okay. It may take us some time to get back, but we'll get there. Sir, now if you would do me one favor."

I said, "What is it?"

He said, "If things go south, never give up on us. Between Chuck, DeLisa, and me and our range finders, we can get out of anywhere."

I said, "I don't think I could give up on you guys, even if I wanted to."

It didn't take long for our conversation to turn to jokes and women and such. We were both laughing and carrying on when DeLisa walked up, looked at both of us, and said, "It's time to break this up. You boys are going to have plenty of time to play." Then looking at me, she said, "I want to go home. Are you ready?"

I said, "Yes, it's time to get out of here."

Getting into my car, DeLisa scooched right up against me and began holding my arm. With her head laying gently on my shoulder, she said, "You're upset at me, aren't you?"

Looking out my driver's side window and gathering my thoughts, I said, "DeLisa, this whole mess we got ourselves into has got me worried, and 'upset' is not the word I would use. I'm disappointed, deeply concerned, and praying both of us get through this next mission alive."

Pulling the car off the side of the road and turning the car ignition off, my emotions were off the charts. Looking at her, I said, "I could lose you on this mission!"

Then I said, "A shooter! Really? How and when did you become a sniper? Do you know what would happen if you were to be caught?

"First, a woman in a 'boots on the ground' operation getting out to the public would rock our world, not to speak of a PR nightmare for the Army.

"Second, if you ever got caught, putting a bullet in my own brain would be appropriate because if I didn't, your dad would.

"Third, subconsciously, I'm so proud of you being the only active Army female sniper. It's almost unbelievable. I have heard of the two shooters with you, and they have both stated to me, 'Don't worry, DeLisa is the best.' Coming from them, that's high praise. Have you been on that many missions for those guys to say you're the best?"

Interrupting my million-mile-per-hour mind and questioning session, DeLisa said, "Okay, okay, okay! When I was recruited, I was on the range in basic training. They saw something in my accuracy on the range and began giving me different scenarios than the other trainees. The targets became more and more difficult as it continued, but apparently, my performance was better than they had ever seen. On the range, I was putting a round in a flea's ass at over 1760 meters. That's a mile! And that was with *no* formal sniper training.

"I did go through E & E (escape and evade) training down in Florida with the teams as a team member after sniper school. The whole training thing was physically and mentally demanding.

"As far as getting caught, you know yourself. There is not a single person who can say how they will handle being interrogated until it happens to them. You also know that nowadays, it's not 'if' someone breaks. It's 'when' they break.

"As far as your concern for me, I can relate. How do you think I felt when you went out on medevac missions knowing you're the one the teams want to extract them from a hot LZ because nobody else has the guts or, should I say, is stupid enough to accept a mission like that? Do you know what the teams call you? They call you the warrior's savior. *I call it the savior who pisses me off!* Knowing you accepted those mission requests when nobody else would and knowing Hoot was the guy I dreamed about spending my whole life with was terrifying for me too. So don't lay your 'deep concerns' crap on me when I'm doing something similar to what you have been doing."

Conceding, I said, "Okay, DeLisa, I see your point, but during those days, I didn't know the love of my life was the same one talking on the radio, and you knew Hoot was me."

Raising my voice slightly, I said, "Now how far do you want to take this?"

Placing her head back on my shoulder, she said quietly, "Rob, just take me home and take me to bed. Being as close to you for the rest of the night is all I want."

I looked at her and asked, "Did we just have our first argument?"

She said, "Yes, but I wouldn't call it an argument. When we get home, let's practice making up!"

I said, "Oh my, sounds good to me."

CHAPTER 6

Get Your Mind Right

One of the hurdles to overcome in preparation for a mission of this magnitude, which has the possibility of a no-return scenario, is the ability to keep the motivation of all the members at a high level during the training phase.

During training, placing the members in a no-win scenario at the beginning demonstrates very quickly who the quitters are. Fortunately, we only had one. He was removed only two days into the training. He was a copilot and did not demonstrate the navigational skills required in the event he had to be in a navigator's role. Before we could help him get his bags packed, Ron had his replacement selected, notified, and inbound to our location the same afternoon. I knew Ron was good, but wow!

When the copilot departed, we only waited about forty-five minutes, and his replacement was standing at the front door, trying to figure out how to get in. Everyone was blown away. As the new guy (The Turtle) checked in with Ron, the remaining pilots were debriefing one another's performances after their flights earlier that day. I was adamant about each pilot being able to say what they wanted to say without reprisal. If we had a possibility of facing a no-win scenario, sometimes, great ideas come from people you would least expect. Having them contribute their ideas increased a positive motivational aspect of the entire mission too, which helped tremendously. It gave them purpose.

Tomorrow night, we would start night-vision-goggle flights commencing at 2300 hours. We designed a route similar to the route we would be flying to our pick-up point. Additionally, we invited our friendly Air Defense Artillery battalion to set up air defense systems along the way to let us know if we're low enough to evade detection. Each aircraft had installed an instrument to let the pilots know if we had been detected or locked on by air defense radar and from which direction it was coming from. This indication would let us know if we needed to get lower or hide to break their radar lock on our aircraft. All three of us pilots were excited to see how we were going to measure up.

As the pilots were finishing up our brief, the two teams came in after their practice today in setting up a continuous retreating maneuver from their package rendezvous point back to the aircraft extraction point. In a very short time, our briefing room started smelling pretty bad; it had been a hot day. Then the door opened, and in walked the three shooters. All three were hot, sweating, and smelled just like us.

All the parties were here, and then Ron walked in. Entering the room, he began making a terrible face and said, "Rob, you need to cut these people loose and go get cleaned up. Man, everyone smells like they've been in the bush for two weeks."

Everyone was laughing and getting well-acquainted. Suddenly, one of the team members noticed that one of the shooters was a female, DeLisa. He said something under his breath, but it was not understandable. I told everyone they were dismissed, and there was a cooler full of beer outside next to the picnic table. Lots of happy yelling and laughing commenced in getting to the beer first. I asked DeLisa and SFC Johnson to stay back; I wanted to talk to them.

I said, "Johnson, do you have a problem working with a female?"

He stated (in a smart-ass type of attitude), "I have never had a female overwatch before, and I am concerned of her abilities to cover my ass."

I began to open my mouth when DeLisa butted in, saying, "Look, you, sorry chauvinistic *pig*, you have no idea of my capabilities. If you did, you wouldn't have opened your mouth at all."

I stood, moving in front of Johnson, and said, "She has more kills than you have total missions, shithead. DeLisa, your dismissed. Go have a beer."

Turning back to Johnson, I said, "I'll give you thirty-six hours to get your head on straight or I'll send you packing. Is that clear?"

Then I said, "No, disregard that. Go get your platoon leader and get him in here now and you need to be here as well!"

As he left, I pushed the intercom button for Ron's phone. He answered, and I said, "Ron, you need to come back here. I think we have an issue with one of the team members."

He said, "Stand by, I'll be right there."

Walking in the door, Ron asked, "What's going on?"

I said, "I have got SFC Johnson coming in with his platoon leader to discuss whether or not SFC Johnson will be with us on the mission or not. He seems to have issue with a female overwatch or a female in general covering his butt."

Ron looked like he was in a *Harry Potter* movie, literally fuming from his ears. He said, "I will take care of this right now!"

The platoon leader and Johnson walked in.

Immediately, Ron jumped all over the lieutenant about his man's attitude towards SFC Lawrence. Ron said, "Lieutenant, you have twenty-four hours to get this man's head right or your entire team is gone. Do you understand that? And you, sergeant, if SFC Lawrence doesn't think you are not the greatest soldier in the world, twenty-four hours from now, you're gone! Is that clear to both of you?"

Ron went on to say, "I have seen SFC Lawrence take almost an entire company of bad guys down from over a mile away. Both of you owe her a huge apology, and it better be sincere. If you have messed with her head in a negative way that affects this mission, I will have both of your asses served up on a silver platter. All I have to do is make one phone call, and your team is gone, and, lieutenant, your career will be finished before it starts."

Ron said, "Mr. Lancaster, you are to report back to me tomorrow afternoon at 1700 hours, letting me know if SFC Lawrence is willing to work with SFC Johnson or not. If not, tomorrow night,

SFC Johnson, you'll be packing your bags. Lieutenant, if he goes, your team may go too. It's going to depend on how well you make your case *to me* in keeping the remaining members of your team here and if they can pick up SFC Johnson's slack. I don't have the time nor the patience for this bullshit. Is that clear? Gentleman, are there any questions?"

The sergeant said, "No, sir."

The lieutenant said, "No, chief."

They were dismissed.

As I looked at Ron, I said, "Wow! Remind me never to piss you off."

He said, "Those guys really make me mad. Hell, DeLisa wouldn't even have been selected for this unless she was one of the best *or the best*."

"I know this kind of guy. You need to keep close tabs on DeLisa. Oh yeah," he chuckled, "please tell DeLisa not to kill him."

I said, "Roger that."

Walking out the door, I saw Johnson sitting at the picnic table, drinking a beer all alone, and the rest of his team together were throwing the football in the front of operations.

Seeing DeLisa standing with her team against my car, drinking a beer, I walked up and said, "How is everybody doing tonight?"

Dave jumped in and said, "We are doing great with these beers. Thank you, sir. We all needed one of these, especially DeLisa. She was ready to take someone out!"

Looking at me, DeLisa said, "I am fine. I hate dealing with *pigs* like that."

I said, "Don't hold back. Tell me how you really feel!"

About a moment after I said that, it felt like my arm was going to fall off; DeLisa slugged me hard right at the top of my arm and said, "Don't be teasing me. I'm not in the mood."

I said, "Yes, ma'am."

Then I felt her hugging my arm, getting close to me, and saying, "It's time to go home."

Looking at her team, I said, "Gentlemen, enjoy the night and stay out of trouble. We will see you tomorrow."

After getting home, our phone rang. When she answered, she looked at me and put it on speaker, desiring me to listen; it was SFC Johnson.

He stated, "I wanted to call to tell you I was wrong to say what I did about you as a woman providing overwatch. From my understanding, you may be the best shooter in the US. Also, I understand you went through the E & E course in Florida. Is that right?"

DeLisa said, "Yes, that's correct. Not only did I go through the course but I also went through the course as part of a SEAL Team. I not only passed but I was also the last one captured, and I was less than thirty feet from the finish line. It took them two and half days to catch me. Johnson, just do me a favor. Stay away from me and do your job. I will do mine, and when this is over, you leave. I don't want you within two hundred feet of me ever."

Johnson said, "That's fair. Wilco and out."

Not saying anything about her comments, I just looked at her and said, "Please be careful out there. If you can make it back to the LZ to depart with the package, I will be truly thanking the Lord. If not, you'll be briefed on an alternate extraction plan. Me and Ron are working on one if any member does not depart on any of the aircraft."

CHAPTER 7

Load Up

1800 hours
    Zero hour - 5: report time for physical check

1900 hours
    Zero hour - 4: equipment check

2000 hour.
    Zero hour - 3: load equipment, preflight aircraft

2100 hours
    Zero hour - 2: issue ammo

2200 hours
    Zero hour - 1: final brief/WX check for go/no-go

2300 hours
    Zero hour: launch

Hoping this day would never come, the night before was a surreal night for DeLisa and me. We both had big jobs ahead of us that would require each of us to perform at 100 percent.

Holding her close in my arms the entire night, I could tell DeLisa was tired from all the training scenarios she had put herself and her team through. I know she was mentally ready for whatever her and her team was going to confront.

Remembering looking at the clock before I passed out, it was a little after four. Feeling the sun on my face and rolling over to hold DeLisa, I found my arms feeling an empty bed and heard some noise in the kitchen. She had awoken, slipped out of bed, and was making us some ham and cheese omelets to start the day. From the bedroom, it smelled so good. The coffee was brewed and contributed to the wonderful aroma of the breakfast she was almost finished with.

Walking toward the wonderful breakfast aroma and leaning against the doorway, watching her work her magic in the kitchen was a moment any man in love would die for. Looking at her from the rear, observing her long legs with just one of my shirts on, the passion was almost overwhelming. She turned around, sensing me behind her; her eyes displaying the art of giving her soul to me and craving my approval tended to make my insides churn with joy but at the same time pure thankfulness. DeLisa continued her culinary magic as I observed in amazement. Her desire to please me, at times, made me wonder, *What did I ever do to deserve such a strong, intelligent, and caring woman?*

It was about 10:30 a.m.; she turned to me, slowly walked over to me, and initiated the most erotic good-morning kiss. Her hand gently caressed the back of my neck, driving me up the wall; she knew it too! Gazing into those never-ending piercing, green eyes, I could see her love and happiness as though it was the night that I had asked her to marry me in the helicopter at Fort Rucker, Alabama. With that look and her seductive kiss, she was definitely teasing me.

Looking at her in total surrender, I said, "Do you want to eat breakfast or what?"

She looked at me while chuckling and said, "Oh, you're going to eat breakfast, mister. I didn't slave this morning for nothing, then we can you know what!"

I laughed, held her tight, and told her, "I love you more now than you could ever imagine."

DeLisa, looking so seriously into my eyes, said, "Let's sit down and eat."

"Sounds good to me. I'm starving," I explained.

As we sat down and was preparing our plates, you could see the German fields out our window. It was another perfect, bright, sunny morning, with just a slight breeze and about 68° outside. Bringing my eyes back inside to DeLisa at the dining table, she still exhibited that serious look I noticed earlier.

I said, "Why so serious?"

She stated, "I wish we had married before this upcoming mission. I have prepared some paperwork for you to put in our special documents safe. You need to know where these things are if something happens to me. Without these documents and us not being married, if any decisions need to be made about my health, these documents give you the authority to ensure you are the one making the decisions and not someone I don't know."

DeLisa was always the one ensuring the future was taken care of for both of us.

I said, "Wow, Dee, I was getting ready to do the same thing. I went to the JAG last week and updated my will, power of attorney, and medical power of attorney. Those documents are already in our safe with 'For DeLisa' marked on the folder."

Observing her eyes again, you could see that her eyes were turning to the seriousness of our upcoming tasks.

I said, "No, we are not going there yet. We have another six hours before starting the count down to zero hour, and I will not let you waste one minute of our time together worrying about what may or may not happen. Is that clear, sergeant?"

Looking at me with those piercing eyes, she dropped her fork in her plate, moved to me, sat in my lap, put her arms around my neck, kissed me, and said, "Now it's time for what!"

After experiencing moments of tenderness with the woman of my dreams, exhaustion finally surrendered to deep sleep.

With both of us falling into a deep sleep, it was fortunate that I had set my alarm for 2:00 p.m. (1400 hours). As comfortable as we were, we would have slept through zero hour.

Packing all our gear and seeing her shooter's robe for the first time, everything started weighing on me now. Placing certain things in small plastic bags and filling her robe pockets, I thought, *She has prepared for every contingency.* It gave me a certain amount of comfort, knowing she was prepared for the worst. Knowing others in her profession respected her greatly was also a comfort to me. But knowing things in a combat situation can go south at any moment did not help me in worrying about her safety. The only thing that gave me comfort was she was going to be at a standoff range of about three-fourth mile when she got into position. Her position was a half mile away from our LZ. I knew she would not cover a half mile in her equipment to make my aircraft departure time after the package arrived. Her only transport out was one of the other two aircrafts that were taking the teams out. Dave was in that same situation. Because of their overwatch positions, their only hope to be extracted was making it back to the LZ or evade making it to our alternate extraction LZ twelve hours later.

With Ron's permission, I had prepared an extraction plan in the event any of the shooters did not make it back to the LZ at departure time. There was no one in the chain of command all the way up who wanted to give the okay in going back across the border to extract anyone who was left behind to begin with. The disdain I had developed for politicians ran deep and emotionally charged at times.

Trying to put all that in the back of my mind and tend to the mission at hand, we packed up our gear in the car and felt we were ready for anything. Looking at my watch, it was half hour to the base, and we didn't have to be there for another two and a half hours. Not wanting to sit around at the base for two hours, looking at DeLisa, I said, "*It's what time!*"

She laughed, ran into the house, and yelled, "You better hurry!"

Running so fast through the front door, there was not another person on earth who could have been any faster. We are talking "warp speed, Captain Kirk, move over!" We both just laid on the bed, holding each other, for at least an hour. Her being so tranquil and relaxed was so obvious; for me to interrupt it would have been, in her mind, an unforgivable offense.

She was in her own little world, lying in my arms. This assignment had the potential to expose the worse possible outcome for me and her, but we had not discussed the possibility of not seeing each other ever again.

Lying on my back, her head on my chest, she suddenly lifted her head, looked at me, and said, "If something happens to me, I want you to go on with your life and be happy."

Placing my finger on her lips, I said, "No, we are not going there. With the people we have on this mission, if the need arises, we could eliminate close to three to four hundred soldiers if the situation demanded. Besides, I do not believe in a no-win situation. You will find that out at the brief."

It was 2200 hours; everyone was in the briefing room waiting for the final mission brief. Everyone checked in, equipment were loaded on the aircraft, personal equipment were checked, and all the ammo were issued.

As Ron and I walked into the briefing room, everyone stood at attention.

Ron blurted out, "At ease. Be seated."

Ron began by saying, "I believe everyone in this room knows everyone. I am Chief Warrant Officer 4 Ron S., and I am the commander and intelligence liaison for this mission."

Pointing at me, he continued to say, "This is Chief Warrant Officer 3 Rob Lancaster. He is our air mission commander (AMC) and executive officer (XO) for this mission."

Ron continued to say, "I shall have full authority to terminate this mission anytime I feel we have been exposed.

"In the event you experience lost communications with the comm center, the decision to terminate the mission will be made by the XO. I will have four operators in charge of communications. Each team leader will have their own dedicated comm center operator.

"Lieutenant—team leader for *Alpha* Team,

"SFC Johnson—team leader for *Bravo* Team,

"SFC Lawrence—team leader for *Charlie* Team, and

"CW3 Lancaster—team leader for *Delta* Team.

"For lost communications, the XO is CW3 Lancaster.

"Once the package, code-named *Geek*, is delivered for extraction, and CW3 Lancaster departs, lieutenant, you will become the air mission commander and XO for the remaining two aircraft and for the duration of the mission. Your mission is to get all team members extracted and across the border by whatever means necessary. We will have an additional two aircraft running and waiting just across the border, ready to provide you with support, if required. Are there any questions?"

Ron went on to say, "Each team member has their map and code names of checkpoints that have been memorized. Does any team member not know all the checkpoint code names?"

Looking at me, he said, "Rob, it's all yours."

Looking at my air crews, I said, "Air crews, your mission is to provide air transport to our designated teams in this room to the LZ known as The Party. The Prom is here at home, and we will be departing at 2300 hours and arriving at The Party at 2402 hours. You will depart under night vision goggles and remain so the entire mission. Flight conditions will be 'clear blue and 22,' no wind and 55°F.

"Delta 1 (Chaulk 1) will carry Charlie Team, and

"Delta 2 (Chaulk 2) will carry Alpha Team, and

"Delta 3 (Chaulk 3) will carry Bravo Team.

"The alternate LZ is The Jail. Check your maps. Ensure its marked correctly.

"Your route is marked on the map, and it is almost identical to the route you have been flying for practice.

"Drawing any small-arms fire or air defense artillery activity will terminate this mission immediately.

"Formation will be 'loose trail at ninety knots.'

"Standard IMC protocol:

"Chaulk 1—straight ahead
"Chaulk 2—30° right
"Chaulk 3—30° left
"Climb to—MSA, three thousand feet

"There are no instrument conditions forecast for tonight, but in the event we encounter IMC and if we climb to three thousand feet, we will be sitting ducks for the Soviet Union's air defense systems.

Additionally, they will launch their intercept aircraft. A Huey is no match for a MiG-25 or a Su-27. We're good, but I don't think we are that good.

"Now for the change in mission parameters.

"In the event one or more team members does not get back to the LZ for extraction for whatever reason, there will be an extraction at 2400 hours the following night on the Oder River due north of a town called Czarnowo. The aircraft will be at the location for twelve minutes, no more. If no one is recovered at that time, located at that same location is a small-but-very-fast raft boat to get you upriver. Continue riding the river until reaching a town called Ratzdorf. You will still be in East Germany, so do not trust anyone. In Ratzdorf is a safe house. The address is in your documents handed out to you. If you are captured, the destruction of the address of the safe house is imperative. At the safe house are people who has assisted our agents many times in the past. They also have communications with our comm center, so you can get word to us you are okay and need assistance. We're not leaving you there under any circumstances. Are there any questions?"

I looked at Ron and said, "Do you have anything else?"

Ron said, "Yes, just one more thing, good luck, watch one another's back. We will see you with the Geek hopefully about 0200 hours."

I said, "Flight crews, we will be engine start in twenty minutes and comm check in twenty-five minutes. Good luck, everyone."

CHAPTER 8

The Mission

All my gear was loaded and secured in the cockpit, and if needed, it was within my reach and easy to move quickly out of the aircraft if egress was required.

Putting my seat all the way down, my copilot looked at me and said, "How in the world do you fly like that? Can you even see over the instrument panel?"

Smiling at him, I stated, "If I can't see them, they can't see me."

We both laughed, and he put his seat down about two more notches.

Laughing, I said, "Okay, checklist, you call, and I'll do."

He said, "Yes, sir."

He read out loud, "Overhead switches and circuit breakers?"

I said, "Set as required."

He continued, "Bat switch?"

I answered, "On."

Continuing and completing the checklist, I looked over my shoulder and saw Scotty giving me a thumbs up. I called "clear," pulling the trigger.

The sound of a Huey starting is unlike any sound on earth. The power of a workhorse is in your one little fingertip pulling the trigger to start an engine with over 1100 hp. Your adrenaline begins to control your thoughts when hearing the sounds of the turbine spooling up.

I observed all the gauges, ensuring they not only come alive but all the needles also go to the right positions, then I heard and felt that distinct sound of a Huey's blade whopping through the air. Feeling the blades turning, turning on all the radios, setting all the navigational equipment, setting the clock, setting the altimeter, and turning to the copilot, I said, "Go ahead and goggle up. I have the controls."

Then he said, "Goggles set. I have the controls."

Relinquishing the controls to him, I said, "Scotty, goggles down?"

He responded, "Goggles down."

Placing my goggles down and making some minor adjustments, I said, "Goggles set. I have the controls. Grab your map. TACAN set. I'll get the comm check."

Switching frequency to FM, I stated, "Delta 2, this is Delta 1 on fox, comm check, over."

Delta 2 responded, "Loud and clear on fox."

"Delta 3, this is Delta 1 on fox, comm check, over."

Delta 3 responded, "Loud and clear."

I said, "Before takeoff check."

My copilot asked, "RPM?"

I said, "6600."

He said, "Systems check."

I said, "All green."

He said, "No caution or warning lights."

Finally, I asked, "Crew, passenger, and mission equipment secured?"

Scotty said, "Secured."

I said, "Clear right."

Scotty stated, "Clear right."

I said, "Clear left?"

My copilot stated, "Clear left."

For just a brief moment, I took a breath and looked at the clock. Pulling the radio talk trigger, I stated, "Delta 2 and 3, Delta 1 is repositioning for lineup and departure."

Pulling the beast off the ground and feeling the aircraft, I said, "Flight control check—normal."

Hovering out to the runway and waiting for Delta 2 and 3 to line up, I felt DeLisa's hand. She was sitting right behind me and had slid her hand between my door and the armrest on my seat, clutching my right arm. Placing my left hand across my body and on top of her hand, I felt her squeeze my arm, and then her touch disappeared.

Hearing Delta 2 and Delta 3 state they were in position and looking at the clock, I stated, "Delta Flight, pitch pull in thirty seconds from mark."

I said, "Mark!"

Pulling the collective up until we were light on the skids, we had about ten seconds before liftoff. When the clock hit five seconds, I started counting down on the radio. "Five, four, three, two, one, liftoff."

After climbing out, I made a radio call. I asked, "Delta 3, this is Delta 1, are we all up?"

I heard "Delta 1, this is Delta 3. All aircraft are up and in staggered right."

I said, "Roger, Delta 3. Flight, execute free trail."

The mission seemed to be starting well and on time. No issues or concerns.

Three minutes out from crossing the border, I said, "Flight, this is Delta 1, executing ninety knots and NOE at mark."

Thirty seconds later, I stated, "Mark slowed to ninety knots and descended to treetop level."

Calling comm center, I said, "Checkpoint Charlie, mark!"

My comm center radio operator said, "Roger report, Bravo."

We were right on schedule with only five minutes before reaching our LZ. Suddenly, we noticed a laser directly ahead in the area of where our LZ should be. That was our forward observer that set up the LZ. We could see the laser from quite a distance.

Making the radio call, I said, "Comm center, this is Delta 1, we have laser green in sight."

The dispatcher stated, "Roger, Delta 1, that's your LZ."

"Delta Flight, this is Delta 1, LZ in site, back to sixty knots on my mark. Mark."

Slowing to sixty knots, we were able to see all the LZ details now clearly.

I said, "Delta Flight, this is Delta 1, reposition to diamond formation on mark. Delta 2, you need to be to the right and 3 should be left. Mark. Maneuver as close to the tree line as you feel comfortable."

The landings were all perfect. No surprises, and no one knew we were there. Calling comm center, I said, "Delta Flight is arrival at The Party. Will be shut down. Delta Flight, this is Delta 1, shut down."

As the aircraft shut down and the rotors came to a stop, both A and B teams were to the front left of the lead aircraft. They were getting ready to depart to the rendezvous point to pick up the Geek.

Chuck had already deployed to the right, Dave was getting ready to deploy in the middle, and DeLisa walked up to my right. My door was open; she stepped onto the skid, grabbed my survival vest, pulling me down, and kissed me hard.

She said, "I love you and will see you back at The Prom."

I said, "Please be careful. No hero shit, okay?"

She said, "Don't worry."

The teams were only supposed to be gone for thirty minutes. It had already been thirty-five. Suddenly, all the flight crews at the LZ heard several muffled shots in the distance. It was definitely one of the shooters' long-range rifles with a suppressor on it. It sounded like it was coming from DeLisa's location. All the flight crews were looking at me, then I knew they were thinking the same thing that was running through my mind. DeLisa was either supplying cover fire for the teams or she was in trouble. In the darkness at the LZ, the quietness was interrupted by the squelch sound of the radio from one of the teams. We heard, "Delta 1, this is Alpha 1, Geek arrival at Party in three mikes, over."

Answering, I said, "Roger, Alpha, Delta 1 will be running."

I said, "Comm center, this is Delta 1, over."

They said, "Go, Delta 1."

I stated, "Geek's arrival at Party in two mikes. Recall Bravo and Charlie to LZ Party, immediate egress for departure in fifteen mikes, over."

Comm center acknowledged and recalled all members to return to LZ for departure in fifteen minutes.

I got strapped in, hit four switches, set the throttle, and pulled the start trigger. The blades started turning; the copilot began turning everything on that was required, set his goggles, and said, "I have the controls."

I said, "Roger, you have the controls."

Setting my goggles, I kept looking for DeLisa to come through the bushes, but it never came to pass.

Suddenly, Scotty said, "Three Alpha Team members and the Geek has arrived, coming up at your two o'clock."

I said, "Roger, get them aboard. We have to depart."

Scotty got them on board, secured them, and said, "We are clear left. Clear right, and everything back here is secure."

The copilot said, "Before takeoff is complete."

I said, "I have the controls, coming straight up."

I told my copilot, "Set my box for comm center frequency on 1, Alpha frequency on 2, Bravo frequency on 3, and Charlie frequency on 4. Put me up on 1."

I said, "Comm center, Delta 1 has left The Party for The Prom as of one minute ago. Did you make contact with all the teams, over?"

I heard "Delta 1, this is comm center, all members of Alpha, Bravo, and Delta members are accounted for. Two members of Charlie Team are located at the party, and there is no contact with the one missing Charlie member. There was no answer on the radio from the missing member."

I said, "Who is it?"

The radio went silent for a moment, and Ron's voice came across the radio and said, "Delta 1, it's Charlie 1."

I said "roger" with a broken voice.

Attempting to never give up hope, I switched frequency to Alpha 1 and said, "Alpha 1, this is Delta 1, if Charlie 1 shows up, notify me as soon as possible, over."

He said, "Delta 1, this is Alpha 1, roger that. We still have ten minutes at The Party."

I asked, "Is Bravo Team ready to launch?"

Alpha 1 stated, "Roger, Delta 3 has the entire Bravo Team on board."

I said, "Launch them. Get them out of there ASAP."

I couldn't hold it back very well; I knew as soon as we heard those muffled shots earlier, the shots were coming from her location. She was in trouble; I could feel it.

As we crossed the border into good-guy territory, we met a C-141 at an air force base. They were waiting for us with more security than I had ever seen. We landed our helicopter in a secure area and were told to shut down. A secure van pulled up next to us, and about six military police jumped out, securing the package and whisking him off in the van to a running C-141. That was the last we ever saw or heard of the Geek.

We were told to sit tight; the MPs would be back to give us a ride to airfield operations. I had time for one more radio call. I said, "Alpha 1, this is Delta 1, over."

There was no answer from Alpha 1, then Delta 2 came on the radio, and I heard "Delta 1, this is Delta 2, Alpha 1 has expired. He is on board. He was hit in the chest. Also, Charlie 1 is on board and pass along to C & C. She took out seven members of a hostile patrol force earlier, protecting Bravo Team. They didn't even know she saved their butts. It was confirmed by Charlie 2. He observed it all. We may not be able to make it out. Troops came out of nowhere when we were launching. I'm doing the best I can in evading missile lock, but it's causing us to be low enough for small-arms fire. We are still nine minutes from good-guy territory, over. Did Delta 3 make it out?"

At that moment, we heard "Comm center, Delta 3, good-guy territory."

I said, "Did you hear that? They are out."

He said, "Roger that. Makes my heart go warm. See you soon. Out."

In the three or four minutes we were shutting down and unloading the package, the remaining three members of Alpha Team, the three members of Delta 2 flight crew, and the three members of Charlie Team had their hands full. The lieutenant (Alpha 1) had been killed, and DeLisa had egressed to the LZ in time to catch Delta 2. I was truly relieved hearing they were on the move.

I kept listening to the radio, expecting to hear Delta 2 calling "in good-guy territory." The call never came.

The MPs came back as they said they would and picked us up, taking us back to the operations building.

As we entered the base operations building, Bravo Team was landing, and we were being led into a situation room.

As we entered the room, I saw more brass in one place than I had ever seen before. My copilot, Scotty, and I didn't know what to anticipate. Suddenly, the monitor came on in the front of the room, and everyone became quiet. The joint chief appeared and began briefing all the brass in the room of what had happened. We had initiated a clandestine mission inside of USSR territory and recovered an asset for President Reagan specifically under the orders of the CIA director.

He went on to say, "Is Mr. Lancaster in the room?"

The 701st military intelligence commander was in the room and said, "Yes, sir, he is right here," as he pointed to me.

The joint chief went on to say, "Mr. Lancaster, you have done this country a great service tonight, and your efforts will not go unnoticed. I understand two-thirds of your team is back now, and you're waiting for the last aircraft to arrive with the final one-third. Is that correct?"

I said, "Yes, sir, we should be hearing from them any minute."

The joint chief went on to say, "Gentlemen, without this piece of the operation, Gorbachev would have never agreed to take down the Berlin Wall."

Many members in the room were never read into the mission, so they were surprised in the fact that they might be a witness to the Berlin Wall coming down during their lifetime. Several members were ecstatic.

I just wanted the rest of my team back. There was a tension building in me due to not being on the radio or hearing Delta 2. I kept looking around to see if anyone was walking into the room. I kept listening to see if I could hear the helicopter land. The silence outside this room was bordering on torture for me.

You could see on the screen the joint chief was interrupted by one of his aids handing him a written message. After looking it over, he said, "Everyone, please clear the room except Mr. Lancaster now, please. That's an order! General, you and the colonel can stay with Mr. Lancaster."

As he continued, he asked, "Are we private now, general?"

The general confirmed we were in a private and secure room.

The joint chief looked up into his camera to us and said, "Mr. Lancaster, I have just been informed your fiancé was a shooter on this mission. Is that true?"

I said, "Yes, sir, she led Charlie Team in an overwatch capacity protecting Alpha and Bravo Team members during the mission."

He stated, "It has been confirmed that she protected Bravo Team by taking out an entire squad that was tracking them back to the LZ." Then, with a big sigh of sorrow, he said, "I am truly sorry to inform you that Delta 2 was shot down six minutes ago, and there appear to be no survivors."

As I sat at the table in disbelief, I could feel a rush of sadness and emptiness consume me instantly like I had never felt before. The emotion ran so deep the inside of me felt as though someone had been kicking my insides for hours. I felt so sick, and my stomach transformed to mush. My head was throbbing to the point my vision was blurred, and I wanted to vomit. My hands and body were experiencing an uncontrollable trembling and quivering with the thought of never seeing DeLisa again.

About that time, I saw Ron walk in the door. Then I knew DeLisa was gone forever. He had been flown up to fly us and my aircraft back to Augsburg knowing I would be in no condition to do so.

As Ron approached, I reached out, and he wrapped his arms around me, and I just lost it. My knees buckled; Ron held me up and supported me back to the chair.

After the meeting, Ron was the person who got me through the next few days of sorrow and anger. He was steadfast in ensuring I was never alone for the first three to four days after the incident.

After about a week, the State Department was able to have all the remains returned. Every one of the bodies required a closed casket. Due to SFC Lawrence (DeLisa) not having any next of kin here in Germany, it was mandatory for someone to be assigned to accompany her remains back to the US and to oversee her funeral arrangements. I volunteered and, considering our relationship, was pleased that the command agreed it would be appropriate for me to perform this function. I took her home and coordinated all the funeral arrangements. Hearing everyone speaking of her in the past tense was an awareness I never anticipated in our relationship. Experiencing difficult tasks in my life and always being able to come through, I truly didn't know if I could do this. This function was, by far, the most difficult tasks of any I had ever encountered. Being the one to give the eulogy at the request of her father took every ounce of strength of every fiber of my being to complete.

I did not want to experience saying goodbye forever until I pass too. Being surprised at my ability to hold it together went totally down the toilet at the burial site. As the casket started to lower, the honor guard began their three rounds of firing salute, and then, saluting, I knew what was coming.

As soon as "Taps" started to play, I lost it. Tears poured down my cheeks like Niagara Falls, my knees began to buckle, and I could feel a soldier on each side of me holding each arm to steady my balance.

In completing the ceremony, it was my responsibility to receive the flag from the pallbearers and take it to her father because her mother had already passed away. As I leaned over, handing her father the folded American Flag, and began to speak, he stood up in front of me, grasped both my shoulders, turned me around, and sat me down in the chair he was sitting in.

He said, "Rob, she would have wanted you to have this. She loved you more than life itself."

Standing up again, we hugged each other in trying to comfort each other in the loss of the love in both our lives. I knew at that moment my heart would be empty for a long time to come.

After everyone had departed the burial site at the cemetery, I ended up remaining there for another five to six hours. The emotions of leaving her there all by herself was playing havoc on my brain for I know she didn't like being all alone.

Hearing something behind me, I turned and looked up; it was the best friend ever, my dad. In his soft but always voice of reason, he said, "Son, she will always love you. You need to get some sleep. By the way, when was the last time you have slept?"

Looking up at him and shrugging my shoulders, I mumbled, "I can't remember."

Putting his hand out for me to take, he said. "Come on, let's get some food in you and let you get some rest."

As we moved further away from her, all I could do was look back at the headstone, thinking, *I really don't want to leave.*

My dad placed his arm around me, leading me to the car. When we pulled away and I could not see her site any more, bowing my head, I couldn't do anything but let the tears flow like God's mightiest rivers. Dad, driving with his left hand on the steering wheel and reaching out, trying to comfort me, with his right hand on my shoulder, actually disrupted my emotions and helped me get through that very stressful and sad moment. Gathering myself a little, looking out the window and rolling it down to get some fresh air seemed to help when taking a few deep breaths.

Maintaining my nonfocused glare out the window, I said, "Dad, thanks for being here. It means everything to me. Do you mind if I close my eyes?"

He said with a deep sigh and his voice with a heavy heart, "Go ahead and relax. We have another thirty minutes to go."

As my eyes gave way to the darkness of exhaustion and being in such a state of enfeeblement, I was oblivious during the remainder of the drive to my father's house. My dad stated later that he had a challenging time in awakening me.

After my dad assisted me to my old bedroom I grew up in, he left me alone to get some well-needed sleep.

The shock of my body shaking and hearing someone calling my name literally made my heart jump almost out of my chest. Being in such a deep sleep for almost an entire twenty-four-hour period, my mouth was so in need of some liquid, and my eyes were filled with the dried crust of past tears. My mind feeling groggy and my eyes still blurry, I tried to stand and ended in a wobbly fall. Landing on my left side and ending up with several bruises did not improve my condition any.

My dad, hearing my fall, came running in and helped me to my feet.

Looking at him, I asked, "Are you sure I have not been on a drunken binge?"

Hearing me make a sarcastic comment, my dad seemed to be happier than before. Helping me up, he said, "Come on, you're going to be all right." He was truly worried about me getting through this because his awareness of my relationship with DeLisa.

Being around my dad for about five days seemed to help begin some of my healing in the emotional disbelief of her loss, but in real life, the emotional hurt never seemed to dissipate.

As time refused to cease in moving forward, the date to return to Germany was arriving tomorrow. Looking back on all the support my father had generously demonstrated during these hard times cemented the bond we had already built.

Now traveling back to the place that DeLisa had passed away happen to be another emotional roller-coaster ride I had never expected to have to confront. It happened to be a stronger emotion than I ever anticipated.

CHAPTER 9

Coping with the Loss

Returning home from the funeral and handling the loss of DeLisa, my heart had begun turning to stone. I arrived back in Augsburg when the funeral had been completed; leaving DeLisa's grave site invoked extreme pain and sorrow. Visiting her every day while I was at home became an emotional requirement for me to have the ability to get through the day. Now she was thousands of miles away.

Recalling before my travel back to Augsburg and trying to piece my life together to continue my flying career, her father had come to my dad's house to encourage me to go on with my life. He stated it was her time for the Lord to take her, and I should be proud that she is in heaven. Through this entire situation, her father had been very supportive. He knew I did not want to go back to Europe and leave the proximity of her resting place, but he assured me her site would be well-taken care of after my departure by him, which gave me great comfort. He also advised me that the longer I stay out of the cockpit, the more difficult it would be to fly again, so, in his opinion, I needed to get back flying as soon as possible.

It took some time for the Army to let me fly again. They were concerned of my mental health in DeLisa passing away. Several months went by with thoughts of literally drowning my sorrows in bottles of scotch and whiskey. I found great comfort in the nightly rituals of toasting DeLisa each night with a glass of Chivas, a Scotch whiskey, I had come to favor very much.

About three months after our mission, in June 1987, President Reagan made a speech near the Brandenburg Gate, calling for Gorbachev to tear down the Berlin Wall. All I could think of was, *If the wall did come down, DeLisa's efforts would not be in vain.*

As time went on and I finally received clearance to get back into the cockpit, the quality of my life seemed to improve as flying gave me a sense of freedom and purpose. The feeling that DeLisa was up there somewhere and watching over me gave me a confidence I never realized before.

Now about two years after her death, on December 22, 1989, parts of the Berlin Wall began being torn down and was finally opened. That night of December 22, along with the feelings of Christmas in just a few days, I found my emotions running deep and strong of the absence of DeLisa. The morning of the 23, I woke up on my apartment floor after a drunken stupor that had commenced the night before, and looking around in a confused state, my Smith and Wesson .45 caliber was on the floor next to me. Not having any recollection of how it got there, an eerie feeling rushed through my body. Picking up the weapon, I thought, *Was I really thinking of using this on myself?* That thought seriously scared me to the bone.

Breaking the silence of my apartment, the ringing of my doorbell helped shake off the cobwebs of my memory loss of last night.

Having to struggle in pulling myself up off the floor and opening the door, Ron looking at me from the hallway didn't seem to be a surprise to me. Ron had been around the world and had experience in many areas of life, including the coping of the death of a loved one. He knew, with Christmas Eve being tomorrow and with the wall starting to come down yesterday, I would not be in good shape. As he entered the apartment, he noticed my weapon on the coffee table right away.

He said, "Look, man, guns and liquor do not go together well. Your weapon is supposed to be locked up in the armory, and that goes for your personal weapons too. It's illegal to have a weapon in

Germany unless authorized by the German government, and you don't have authorization."

Saying that, he grabbed my .45, took the magazine out, and cleared the weapon. He gave me the magazine and the cleared cartridge and said, "Put those bullets up, and I'll turn this in for you. Go get a shower, and I'll wait. You're coming over to my house tonight."

I knew Ron was looking out after me, but I was not in the mood for socializing at this time. As I started to pour another shot, I said bluntly, "Ron, I'm not in the mood right now, so leave me alone."

Ron took my bottle of Chivas and poured it down the drain, saying, "If I have to put you in the shower myself, I'll do it. Now go get cleaned up! *Now!*"

Gathering myself and praying I made it to the shower, I stood beneath the running water; some of my senses began to emerge. Being so exhausted, my body just melted to the shower floor with the water running down my head and to the rest of me. With every ounce of strength in me, I pulled myself back up and began to feel some of my body movement again and started to clean myself up.

After my shower and realizing the need for a shave was evident, I commenced in spreading the shaving cream on my face and looked in the mirror. I said to myself, "How am I going to shave considering I can't even make out who I'm looking at?"

Beginning to laugh loudly at myself, Ron came running in, thinking something had happened. It had; they call it starting to sober up. Being able to think now, even if it was just a little bit, was really helpful to me and especially Ron.

Throwing some clothes on and walking out to the living room, Ron was sitting and talking to someone on the telephone. He looked up at me when I came out of my room with the phone still stuck in his ear; he said, "Rob, I think the 701st Military Intelligence is being shut down. The Department of Army (DA) has already closed all the listening sites we had on the border. The politicians and those gutless Army commanders in their infinite wisdom stated, 'Since the wall came down and the Cold War is coming to an end, it is against the law to spy on your friends.'"

Those were the most untrue statements ever heard by my ears. Those words did not go over well with me at all and, as I stewed on them, made my heart harden even more.

In my opinion, just because the wall came down did not mean we're all going to hug one another and start swapping spit. Now the State Department bureaucrats, taking these events too far as they always did, were looking at closing the entire Augsburg Military Intelligence Base, thus leaving Europe in its entirety, with no early warning of the Soviet Union's possible incomprehensible actions in the future.

I trusted the Russian government, their Spetsnaz and the KGB, about as far as I could spit. There were people in that country who wanted to do nothing but to wipe the United States off the map and would do anything to complete their objective. I was very suspicious of this entire situation. This was not a time to let our guard down, no matter what happens in the USSR. Gorbachev was having some challenging times in converting his country and bringing in capitalism.

Not having any compassion at all about the Soviet Union people and the difficult times they were going through did not disturb me at all. My heart was made of stone for any person I met from Russian descent. The thought that they were the ones who shot DeLisa's aircraft down was always on the forefront of my mind. The anger that had developed within my heart, not being visible on the surface of my expressions, was enormously apparent once my mouth opened. There was no misunderstanding anyone had of my thoughts of the USSR or anyone who initiated policies that placed us in an inferior position militarily. Many of the people making these decisions were playing politics by appeasement. I sincerely had a difficult time in comprehending placing the United States at risk as our fifty-year-old adversary demonstrated one single task of tearing down the Berlin Wall and saying "they want peace."

But being a soldier first and obeying orders of the people above my pay grade were what I was being paid to do. Out of nowhere, all the pilots began receiving orders of transfer to new assignments. Ron received orders for Japan at the military intelligence site in Tokyo. Of all the people leaving, he was the one I really didn't want to see leave.

Finally, I received a call from the assignments branch at Third Army headquarters. I was notified that I had a choice of being an instructor pilot in the 82nd Airborne Division at Fort Bragg, North Carolina, or go to the Berlin Brigade and stay in Germany for another three years.

Being in Europe for more than a total of four years now, in the Far East for five years, and in Central America for one year, the time for me to go home to the US was now. I had two and a half years left before I could retire and had developed a voracious desire in having my feet on the "good old USA" soil.

With DeLisa gone for two years now, the emotion of loneliness began creeping into my sole periodically in lieu of being an everyday event. Even years after her passing, the ability to fill the hole in my heart seemed evident that it would be an impossible feat. The empty hole would always be reserved for my memories of her. The idea of flying in an area (East Germany) in close proximity of where DeLisa was killed did not settle well with me.

Choosing the transfer offer by the assignment branch to go to the 82nd Airborne Division seemed to be the right move at that time. Notifying the assignments branch of my choice they had given me, the Army initiated the process for the orders to be cut and sent to me through the command channels.

All the pilots who were assigned to the Aviation Detachment had been given their orders and had departed. I was the last pilot to leave. Saying all the goodbyes to close friends like Scotty became sad events. We exchanged our permanent addresses so we could stay in touch in the future, but there was much sadness surrounding the detachment considering all we had been through. The number of people who stopped in to see us one last time before closing the doors forever was very surprising.

CHAPTER 10

The Letter

The day came for me to depart the detachment, and the brigade commander came in to wish me much success in my new assignment. He knew many people in the 82nd. He seemed very sincere in wishing me success in the future. He didn't have to come to the detachment to see me off at all, but I believe he wanted to make sure I had recovered after the loss of DeLisa and had no ill feelings of "the mission."

I stated to him, "Sir, all is good."

We parted ways and wished each other success in our future endeavors.

Jumping in a friend's car with my bags packed, we departed Augsburg, Germany, for the Frankfort Airport where I had to catch my flight to Charleston Air Force Base, Charleston, South Carolina.

After checking my bags and checking in with the gate agent to get my seat assignment, I sat waiting for the announcement for the boarding to begin. I noticed the envelope DeLisa had secured in our safe was sticking out of my small bag; I had never opened or read the information in the envelope due to the pain I knew it would cause me. Finally, but with much hesitation, it might be a good time for me to look over what she had placed in the envelope.

Finding a letter she had written was a surprise. I knew all about the legal documents that her father and I had already gone through, but I had not in the past two years come across a letter inside of the envelope. Not knowing if I should read it now or not became a big dilemma. I took a chance on the possibility of overwhelming emotions taking over me while flying on an aircraft probably was not a good idea.

After boarding and settling in my seat and suddenly experiencing a strong desire to open the letter, I took a deep breath as we started our rollout for takeoff. Looking at the folded-up letter, I could feel the wheels retract and lock up in the aircraft. Glancing out the window, I could see a beautiful sunset we were flying into. Recalling on several occasions the way DeLisa enjoyed her sunsets, I took that as a sign from her and began to unfold her letter. Observing the letter being written with the caring love only she could convey was already capturing from me the deepest yearning to hear her voice again. Knowing her piercing, green eyes had always touched my heart, I began to read her letter to me with an unrelenting intensity I had never exhibited.

> *My Dearest Rob,*
>
> *As I write this in green ink, I know you will know why.*
>
> *I am not physically with you anymore, but I pray that I am in your heart forever. In spirit, I will never leave your side.*
>
> *Thinking about the time you first kissed me in the hallway at school, I can't tell you how surprised I was at that moment. But at the same time and at that very same moment, I was praying for that very kiss to occur. Your kiss that day proved to me beyond any question you were the one for me then and for always. That sweet gentle and telling kiss made me want to melt in your arms completely. Your courage was astonishing; it was like we were reading each other's minds. For us, when we were together, reading each other's thoughts seemed to be a natural occurrence. The thought of us losing the opportunity of being together for all those years saddened me so*

much. I cannot apologize for my mother's actions enough. The time we did spend together was better than most couples have together their entire lives, and I thank you for your deepest felt love for me all those years. I could feel your love for me even when I was not with you.

You made my life so fulfilling in every way. I know you're going to be lost with me not being by your side, but please, please, please do not become a hermit and close yourself off to the idea of loving another. Your heart is big enough for me and for you to share your joy and happiness with someone who can make you happy. I know your sense of chivalry and honor tells you not to love someone else, and I want you to please get past those feelings for your love is too precious not to be shared with someone.

I will see you again when the Lord says it's time. Being with you was always the best moments of my life. I will never forget how you never forgot what we had in school and you not ever actively pursuing anyone for a relationship for so many years. That type of dedication only exists if the love you have for someone truly exists.

I remember when I turned around while in a strange land, and seeing you standing behind me after not seeing or being with you for more than eleven years was so heart-stopping for me. I remember your expression too. You were floored. Touching you for the first time after being apart for such a long time was unlike any fantasy a mortal could ever endure. I actually thought I was going to pass out. Holding you again was unbelievably warming.

Rob, I never felt any more in love with you than the night you asked me to marry you. I cannot describe the joy in my heart. For you to go through all the trouble of acquiring the aircraft, having your friends fly us, and talking me into playing dress-up in my formal dress blues was an incredible accomplishment. The pride and love I had for you after that night could never be wavered. In fact, many times after that event, I asked myself, "What did I do to deserve you?" To this day, I can't answer that question. All I can say is the Lord wanted us to share our love and to show others what real love is.

I love you with all my heart.

DeLisa

Folding the letter up again and placing it against my cheek, I leaned my head against the pillow and the window of the airplane. Dosing off, all I could do was to dream of the in-depth emotions I experienced in being close to DeLisa. Reading the letter seemed to provide me with some needed closure and a warm feeling of comfort and protection with her looking over me. For a few moments, I felt the sorrow and loss, then, as I read her letter, I could hear her voice reading the letter to me in my conscience. As I listened to her imaginary voice, a warm satisfaction had conjured up in my stomach knowing she was happy when we were together.

I thought, *She was so right when it came to the thought of me finding someone else.* Not knowing I would ever have the strength in loving someone else besides her was a thought far from my current reality. Even now, after two years of her death, it was unbelievable to think I would not see her again in my lifetime. But after reading her letter, it made me feel it was time to try to reinvent my life and move on.

After landing in South Carolina, during the process of plane debarkation, my name "Rob" was being yelled by another passenger. I moved over into a vacant seating area and started letting the passengers behind me go by so the young lady screaming my name could catch up to me. She was waiving a folded-up piece of paper in her hand, and I suddenly recognized it. It was DeLisa's letter. Seeing the young lady's efforts in getting the letter to me and the thought of misplacing the letter brought an overwhelming feeling of humbleness, and thanks to that lady.

As she came closer, I moved over to the window seat so she could move out of the aisle, allowing the remaining passengers to pass by.

Stepping in front of me and handing the letter to me, she said, "I didn't mean to read it, but when I was trying to find out who's letter it was, her writing had me so mesmerized. By the time I finished, I was a crying wreck. I am assuming you are the Rob in the letter."

I said, "Yes, ma'am, and I can't express my thanks to you for returning this letter to me. It is the most important thoughts she had before passing away."

Sitting down in the seat, I began to place the letter across my face.

As she observed me, she asked, "Are you going to be all right?"

I said, "Yes, she has been gone for about two years now, and I only found this letter about ten hours ago."

She went on to say, "What you two shared was more special than life itself. The experiences you must have had between you two must have been so very heart moving, but you know in your heart what she had alluded to in her letter, getting beyond these episodes and moving on are something you are still going to have to deal with. You have not dealt with that yet, have you?"

Looking into her eyes and noting a genuine and empathetic understanding of my emotions, I said, "For you to return this letter to me is truly fate at its finest. There are no words to express my gratitude. There are people waiting for me, and I must leave at this time. Again, thank you with all my heart, but I have to say goodbye."

While sliding out to the aisle and joining the back of the line to get off the airplane, she turned around and gave me a small piece of paper. She stated, "If you need someone to talk to, I'll be here. Here is my number, and my name is Susannah."

Walking off the plane and down the walkway to the terminal, it felt warm and comforting being back on US soil. I had arranged for a friend to meet me and take me to the car dealership where I had purchased a car about six weeks ago in Germany. Being notified by the dealership that they had received delivery of my car, I gave them the time I would be in to pick it up the next day.

Receiving a call from my friend, he stated he couldn't meet me today but could pick me up tomorrow. His unit had an unexpected briefing by their commander on an upcoming tasking, and I should go ahead and get a hotel room.

I told him I understood and made my way out the terminal door so I could catch the hotel shuttle going to the Holiday Inn. Walking out of the terminal door and carrying what felt like my entire estate on my back, I dropped one of my bags. Frustrated, I just flopped the others down next to it.

"Hey, Rob, need a lift?" I heard from a familiar voice. It was Susannah, the girl I met getting off the plane.

I said, "Yes, sounds good, my friend isn't going to make it until tomorrow."

She said, "You can stay at my place tonight, if you want."

Being a little stunned that she would offer a stranger to stay at her place after meeting them for less than ten minutes was way out of my comfort zone, so I said, "Thanks, Susannah, I better not. I have got so many things to get done tomorrow. If you could just drop me at the Holiday Inn, I would truly be thankful."

Noting that this young lady was fairly stunning, and it wasn't that jumping in the sack with her would not have been most likely out of this world, but there was something intangible that just didn't add up. Putting your finger on something you can't feel, smell, or taste will test your nerve, especially when your gut is telling you to run and fast! So I did.

Being exhausted, I decided to go ahead and get a hotel room for the night. Checking into my room and sitting in front of the television, I was finally able to relax from being wound up from the flight and the time zone change.

About 1:00 a.m., my body yielded to a deep sleep.

At 8:00 a.m., my room phone rang, and it was my friend, wondering if I was going to eat breakfast.

I said, "Yes, I'll be down in about twenty minutes."

After my shower and getting dressed, my wallet fell off the desk, expelling several articles that were in it, including a picture of DeLisa. Looking at it, a warm, flushed feeling came over my body that I had not experienced in quite a while. Knowing the emotion well, I could feel the swelling of tears in my eyes. Pushing the picture back into my wallet and forcing myself to breathe deeply, it helped in getting through the sorrow that was taking over my heart and soul. The reading of her letter on the plane helped immensely in supporting me getting through these moments in time of yearning for her touch.

Opening my hotel room door to the hallway, I could feel the coolness of the hotel air, which also assisted me in regaining my composure. Seeing my friend and feeling very comfortable being back on US soil triggered those wonderful and safe feelings I would experience when being held by DeLisa.

Shrugging the feeling off and sitting down at the table, out of the blue, my friend asked, "How are you getting along?"

Knowing what he was getting at, I said, "It's been hard, but I think I'm going to be all right."

My friend expressed his concern by stating, "I was worried after the funeral, wondering if you were going to be okay. Please don't feel that you can't talk to me about anything, brother. I'm here for you anytime or anywhere."

I told him, "I had some tough days, but I had a friend by the name of Ron in Germany, and he truly helped me through some of the toughest days I had ever faced."

It was nice to walk into a restaurant and have the ability to order a good old Southern breakfast in lieu of something called a "continental breakfast" that didn't fill anyone up. It was another soothing sensation that I had missed for a long time.

My friend and I laughed and carried on for about two hours, and it was time for me to start heading toward Fort Bragg. He understood and agreed it was time for him to start heading back home too. He dropped me at the car dealership so I could pick up my car, and then he departed.

CHAPTER 11

The Best of Times and the Worst of Times

J ust sitting, looking out the window at the dealership, and realizing I didn't have to report to Fort Bragg for another twenty-seven days, I decided to mosey over to Fort Stewart to see if any of the old gang was still there. Only being an hour away, it didn't seem to be out of my way at all.

Making my way down I-95 to Savannah and then cutting across the back roads through the ranges into Fort Stewart, I discovered I didn't miss a beat. It seemed that nothing had changed. Coming into Fort Stewart proper, then taking some back roads to Wright Army Airfield where my old medevac unit was located put me right outside the medevac operations building.

Driving up to the operations building and already feeling at home, the two pilots standing on the porch recognized me and yelled out, "Rob, is that you?"

I walked up to them. Shaking their hands was a warm feeling, knowing friends from your past were doing well.

The commander heard the commotion on the outside porch and came out to see what was going on. Seeing me, he said, "My Lord, it's Rob Lancaster. How are you doing? You know you're a legend around here, don't you?"

I said while chuckling slightly, "Sir, not a legend, I assure you," then I asked, "Sir, how are you doing? You keeping all these guys in line?"

He said yes and asked if I wanted a cup of java. I told him that was why I stopped by. I knew he would offer me a free cup. We laughed, and I followed him into his office. It felt like returning home, but several of my friends had transferred out or had retired.

The commander seemed legitimately happy to see me. Looking at me, he said, "Have you considered coming back to medevac?"

I stated emphatically, "I would return to medevac in a minute! I have had a rough two years in Europe. Some of the situations were continuations of my days in Honduras, and it's been hard to deal with. Now that I'm back in the US, it feels good.

"Wherever I get assigned, they need to know I only have a little over two and a half years to go before I can retire, which I plan on doing."

Continuing my conversation, I told the commander, "I currently have orders to report to the 82nd Airborne Division at Bragg, and I'm supposed to report in about twenty-five days. I didn't really want a frontline division assignment, but sometimes, people are dealt those kinds of cards. I mean someone has to do it, right?"

Looking at me and scratching his chin, he asked, "If I could get your assignment changed to return to the 498th Medevac, could you live with that and be happy?"

I said, "Oh my, sir, I'd be on cloud nine!"

At that point, he told me to take my coffee over to operations and say "hello" to the guys while he made some telephone calls and talked to some of his peeps. In other words, "get the hell out of my office so I could try to get your orders amended."

What I didn't know was his current unit instructor pilot who replaced me after I had departed had family from Fayetteville, North Carolina, that was right outside Fort Bragg. He had told the commander on several occasions that he wanted to return to Fort Bragg one day.

Walking into operations was like old home week. Guys I had known for years were joking and smoking, having a good time, and began telling me all the crazy things that had occurred since I had left. It ended up to be an entertaining and pleasurable day.

The operations officer came in and told the current instructor pilot, "Hey, the commander would like to talk to you in his office."

He said, "Roger that, on my way."

I had known the operations officer for a long time, and glancing at him, he nodded his head for me to come into his office. As I followed him to his office, he asked me if I wanted a refill on my coffee, and obviously, I told him, "I have only had three cups this morning, so I'm authorized at least two more."

He laughed and said, "You haven't changed a bit. That coffee's going to kill you one day."

I said, "Yes, sir, and I am going to go out as a satisfied guy, at least in my stomach."

Then he looked at me strangely and asked, "Weren't you in the recruiting command before you went to flight school? Because I think we received something for you after you left for Germany. It was a letter sent here from Galveston Recruiting Station. We forwarded the letter to the 701st in Augsburg, Germany, but it came back, so I put it in your old file. Do you want it?"

I said, "Yes, sir, let me see who it's from."

Glancing at the return address, I zeroed in on SSgt Linda Johnson's name, the female recruiter who worked for me in Galveston. The envelope was a recruiting envelope from the station and had the telephone number on it. I looked at the operations officer and asked him, "Sir, is there a telephone somewhere I could use to call the Galveston Recruiting Station?"

He said, "Sure, go ahead and use this one. I'll give you the office for some privacy."

I said, "Thanks."

Catching Linda at the same recruiting station would be a long shot for sure. If she had been a successful recruiter, she was most likely at a more demanding station by now, and if she was unsuccessful, she had probably been replaced and would have been sent back to the Army somewhere.

73

Listening at the ring of the telephone, a SSgt Valdez answered. Informing him who I was and who I used to be, I asked if SSgt Johnson was still around. He told me I was really lucky because today was her last day in recruiting. She was leaving the Army. He couldn't give me her number, but I could give him mine, and he would pass it to her so she could call me back. Asking him when she was expected back, he said, "It's going to be late. She is bringing back two guys from Houston who enlisted in the Delayed Enlistment Program. They probably have not finished yet. Do you want me to call her in Houston and tell her to call you now?"

I said, "Sarge, that would be outstanding! Please give her this number. I'll be waiting."

Telling the operations officer what was going on, he said, "Just go ahead and use my office for whatever. Oh, by the way, the commander just told me our current IP wants to go to Bragg. Are you going to take his place?"

At that very moment, his telephone rang, and answering it, I said, "498th Med Company, this is Mr. Lancaster. How may I help you?"

All I heard was Linda's excited voice. "Oh my god, is it really you? Rob?"

I said, "Linda? You sound just the same. How are you?"

I gave the operations officer a thumbs up, and he backed out of the office, closing the door behind him.

Continuing to give my full attention to Linda on the phone, I said, "I heard you are leaving the Army. Is that true?"

Linda went into the bad luck she had suffered through with her new husband after I had left. Her unfortunate calamity with her married life seemed to have overflowed into her professional life in recruiting. After her divorce, she couldn't get the old *mojo* attitude to be that self-starting salesman needed to be an Army recruiter.

She was unaware of how DeLisa and I found each other again while in Honduras and of DeLisa's death in East Germany.

She said, "Okay, I get out in five days, and I am going to come and see you. You got that, mister?"

I told her I would love to spend some time with her. "But please be aware, I am a different person."

She said, "Tell me, what's changed, Rob? I can hear you're troubled." Jokingly, she said, "Are you married?"

Telling Linda DeLisa and I had found each other in Honduras and then our travels to Europe and of the engagement, she went silent. Then she said, "I know you two have to be the happiest people in the world. Why don't you sound like the happiest guy in the world?"

Then as I began the chronicles of Delisa's death, I was barely able to explain to Linda about the feelings being carried by me of DeLisa on the telephone. Having to stop occasionally to compose myself, Linda could hear the sadness in my voice, even over the phone.

She said, "Rob, I can't imagine what you have gone through. I will be there as soon as I can. I know you need someone to just be able to listen to you right now. Go ahead and start looking for a place to live, but don't sign anything until I get there, okay?"

If anyone knew the depth of the relationship between DeLisa and myself, it was my dad, DeLisa's dad, and Linda.

Continuing the conversation and letting Linda know what I was doing at Fort Stewart, she began to open up a little and said, "Rob, I am not asking to take DeLisa's place. I'd be a fool to try and do so. My only intent is to take care of you the best way I can. I have never forgotten how caring you can be. Just being around you is so gratifying for me."

I thought, *She sounds so much like DeLisa's letter it's scary.*

My mind working at the speed of light again, I said, "Okay, I am speaking to the commander in a few minutes. Him, the Department of Army, and the Assignments Branch are determining whether or not the current instructor pilot and me can exchange places. See, I am supposed to go to the 82nd Airborne Division at Bragg at the end of this month. There is this guy here right now who is their current IP, but he wants to go to Bragg, so we are trying to switch."

I said, "Give me your number, and I will call you when you get back from Houston."

She gave me her number. We said our goodbyes, and she reiterated, "I will be there as soon as I can."

The operations officer stated that the Assignments Branch had decided, and the commander wanted to see me. Nervously, I walked over to his office, and knocking on the old man's door, he said, "Enter."

As I entered, I stood at attention in front of his desk and stated, "Sir, Mr. Lancaster, reporting as ordered, sir."

He looked at me and said, "Rob, please sit down. The Warrant Officer Branch and Assignments has approved the switch between you and CW2 Miller.

"*But!* I need to ask you one question. You are one of the greatest pilots I have ever had the pleasure of knowing, and I do not want my younger inexperienced pilots taking on difficult missions they can't handle. I am afraid their ego in trying to impress you may dominate their decision to decline a mission when it should be turned down. How can we keep that from happening and them getting themselves and their crews killed?"

I said, "Sir, the only way to fix that is to make them aware of that very scenario. If we suspect certain pilots taking chances, when we know they shouldn't be, it's not uncommon to suspend a person from being a pilot in command until they learn proper decision-making skills. We make the briefing sheet very stringent in a manner the criteria must be met prior to launch. If it's not, they are prohibited from launching. I can make that brief sheet in about one hour."

The commander said, "That's okay. Complete it when you get back on duty here at Fort Stewart, and congratulations! Welcome aboard, Rob."

Upon departing his office, CW2 Miller was waiting outside the door for the same news I just received. He seemed to be just as pleased as I was.

Walking back over to Operations and talking to the operations officer, I said, "Sir, you're going to have to keep that coffee fresh for me, brother!"

Captain Smith, looking at me and realizing I was his new instructor pilot, began to grin from ear to ear. About four other pilots in Ops heard the news, and they all started shaking my hand and began laughing, telling jokes, and demonstrating this occurrence as a joyful event. Boy, if they only knew how I was going to bust their butts! I just grinned and shook their hands in joy and happiness. Turning and observing the expression on Captain Smith's face, he was just shaking his head and smiling, knowing the pilots had no clue of what they were getting ready to face.

CHAPTER 12

The Air Crew's Awakening

Linda had not arrived yet, and I had already found two apartments and two houses to rent. I knew Linda did not have employment as she just terminated her Army career. In calculating a payment for my new domicile, I did not plan any funds coming from her pocketbook. I believe Linda to be the type of woman not desiring to stay at home but to want to forge out some sort of challenge to make herself successful. She didn't realize how driven she could be until I came along.

I remember her in two different roles: First, when I first met her in the recruiting station, she was timid, shy, and had a definite lack of confidence. After working with her self-esteem and confidence level, she began not only to be a confident person at her job but also a leader unafraid in selling ideas she thought were good ideas.

I was very interested in discovering which woman was going to show up when she arrived.

In the meantime, the day came for my first introductory meeting with the entire Warrant Officer Corps of the 3rd Platoon, 498th Medical Company (air ambulance). They had six aircrafts, three officers, and fourteen warrant officers. In addition, we had seven crew chiefs/mechanics, eight flight medics, and one supply sergeant.

Of the thirty-three members making up the Medevac Platoon, thirty-two were actual crew members who would require documented training by the unit instructor pilot or (IP), and that would be me. I would have the authority to provide class instruction, provide actual flight instruction, conduct flight evaluations, and recommend to the commander who should or should not be a pilot or a pilot in command. I would also be able to implement any policy recommendation to the commander for approval for any and all medevac flight operations.

This authority extended for all crew members, including all the three officers. Most of the medevac flights currently and in combat situations were conducted by the warrant officers, but periodically, I would run into an officer who had superior aviator skills. In those cases and depending on their duty assignment, I would assign them to a combat crew assignment if the commander approved it and if they felt they had the time to train for the position. Captain Smith was truly one of those officers. When I left the unit before going to Germany, I remember him as being one of the top five pilots in the unit.

Before my meeting, I had gone to the G-2 to be read in on what our unit's contingency plans were. Every unit in the Army has a contingency operations plan in the event of war. They train for that contingency plan. The 498th contingency plan was to provide medical evacuation support to the division deployed for any Middle East operations. I needed to develop my training and classes for desert and high-altitude operations. I know the past IP had not done this. Very few were even aware of the contingency plans.

After briefing the commander, the operations officer, and the first lieutenant of our contingency plans on file at G-2 (intelligence branch), the commander agreed we were behind the power curve in these specific types of training scenarios and with this type of operational expertise.

Speaking up, I said, "Sir, don't worry about where our units capabilities are currently. I am devising an eight-week plan to get us up to combat-ready status based on these contingency requirements. In eight weeks from the end of this week, we can have at least six combat crews ready with the expertise to conduct operations that are required and stated within the contingency operations plan on file at

G-2. I plan on providing a list of required training to Captain Smith by the end of this week."

The commander stated, "Mr. Lancaster, there is no question in my mind that this unit came away with the right IP. I am ecstatic that you are with us and looking forward in being combat-ready."

I also stated, "Sir, I have my warrant officer introduction meeting today at 1400 hours. I would like to speak to the warrants by themselves for about thirty minutes prior to all the flight crew members coming in for our meeting at 1430 hours, if I may."

The commander said, "You are our senior warrant officer, and if you can improve the leadership capabilities of our Warrant Officer Corps, I'll let you have all the meetings you want. Gentlemen, I think that's a wrap. Does anyone have anything else?"

Walking out the old man's office, Captain Smith looked at me and said, "Dude, you've been busy."

I said, "Not as busy as those warrant officers over there are going to be. Sir, I am happy that we have known each other for quite a while, and you know what kind of guy I am. I believe you need to expect the possibility of one or two warrants coming to you, complaining about me training too much or me pushing them a little too hard. I want to assure you right now. I will not push them into any training that I have not completed myself or that I feel they can't master."

Captain Smith said, "Yes, I have known you for a while, and no other IP I have known in this entire division has taken the time to research with G-2 the contingency of their own unit. I am totally impressed. You do what you need to do, and I will support you 100 percent."

I said, "Thank you, sir, two bags four."

And off I went to the warrant officer meeting scheduled in ten minutes.

Walking into the room where all the warrants were supposed to be and being perfectly dressed in my flight suit, ready for any type of flight duty, I noticed that many of my fellow warrants would not pass my standards of presenting themselves as a warrant officer in this or any other unit.

Arriving at the front of the room, I said very calmly, "Gentlemen, I am going to walk out of this room and come back in. When I walk in, every 'swinging Richard' in this room better get to their feet at attention as the senior warrant officer has taken his valuable time out of his day to address his new fellow warrant officers. Is that clear?"

I walked out the room and into Operations, and Captain Smith looked at me and started to laugh.

I said, "*Shhhh!*"

Captain Smith knew exactly what I was doing and said, "I am so happy to see you back. This is great!"

Walking back into the room, all I heard was a bunch of feet slamming onto the floor, and looking out, I saw all the warrants at attention. Trying to keep from smiling, I said very loudly, "What are you guys doing? I am a fellow warrant officer. I'm not your commander. Sit your asses down and pay attention."

As they sat, several of the older warrants started chuckling.

"How many in this room have annual evals due in less than eight weeks?"

Three raised their hands, and I told them to see me after this meeting.

I said, "Okay, who here is a night vision goggle (NVG) pilot in command (PIC)?"

Five raised their hands.

"And who here is a PIC but not an NVG PIC?"

Three raised their hands.

I asked those three how long had they been a PIC.

All of them had been a PIC for more than eight months.

I asked, "Is there a reason you are not an NVG PIC?"

Two stated they had been trying to schedule training but without success.

Looking at the third, I asked, "And why aren't you a NVG PIC? You happen to be a CW3 just like me."

He said, "I am retiring in about ten months, and I am not really interested in becoming a NVG PIC."

I stated, "Mister, that is an unacceptable excuse. You are either in the Army or you're not, and you're not within six months of retirement either, so you cannot play that card with me either. By you not being NVG PIC qualified, you're putting a burden on the other PICs to make up your duty shifts, and I am not going to stand for it. From this very moment, I am recommending to the commander that your PIC status be rescinded, and your duty will be as a copilot only. I would like to discuss your options at 0800 hours tomorrow morning in my office. Do you have a problem with that?"

Everyone in the room knew I meant business at that point. Exposing the mediocrity of a senior warrant in our midst demonstrated to all the warrants in the unit, young and old alike, I was not going to accept mediocrity.

Before the meeting adjourned, I laid out my expectations of what I expected of a warrant officer in this unit and what was not tolerable anymore. I also indicated that all warrants who were not on duty was to participate in PT at 0630 hours.

Captain Smith knew I would find someone to make an example out of, so after my "come to Jesus meeting" with all the warrants, I wrote up a negative personnel report on the CW3, placing one copy in his file and the other I carried over to the commander.

The old man approved and signed it and said, "Are you sure you want to do this?"

I said, "Yes, sir, he is hurting the unit and reducing the expertise this unit has, but most of all, by him not being or wanting to be an NVG PIC, he is placing your flight crews at risk. I consider that an unacceptable risk when there is no call for it and especially when the training is available for him. He just does not care, and that attitude is like a rotten apple in the barrel. That's not going to happen on my watch."

About four days went by, and my training schedule had been completed. I had been evaluated by the Regimental Standardizations IP and had passed with flying colors. My office was assembled the way I wanted it, and one of the W-1s had been tasked by me to make a standardization status board. All the flight records had been reviewed, and the noted corrections were being addressed.

Hearing a knock on my door, I said, "Enter," and in walked Linda.

She said, "Linda Johnson reporting for duty, sir."

Laughing, she met me halfway around my desk as I stood. Her arms were being thrown around my neck, and me hugging her was like the hug I had felt when I departed Galveston. Almost forgetting how wonderfully soft she felt and discovering again how gorgeous she was at this moment in time, hugging her raised some of the deep and hidden emotions I had for her years ago. Feeling her need to be against me, she could feel my need for her to be touching me also. Not letting go of her hand and her not letting go of my arm, looking at her blue, needy eyes was like a second moment in my life when I looked into DeLisa's eyes before I kissed her the very first time.

Leaning closer to her, I said, "I can't tell you how much it means to me for you to be by my side."

Her eyes gently closed as her face moved toward mine. I closed my eyes, and the touch of her warm, soft lips on mine was as close to heaven as anything could be.

Looking at her, I said, "I have a room at the guest house, and I have four places for us to look at. Two are apartments, and two are houses to rent. Let's drop your things off at the guest house, and I will take tomorrow off so we can start looking. Does that sound good?"

She said, "Sounds perfect, just a couple of things. First, do you plan on dinner soon? Because I am starving, and second, how many beds are in my guest quarters?"

I said, "If there is more than one bed, we can try them all. How's that?"

Looking at me with a big smile, she said, "Do you think you can keep up?"

Laughing, I said, "Come on, let's eat."

Stopping on the way out, I informed Captain Smith of my day off the next day and introduced Linda to him.

He said, "Take what you need. Just keep me informed."

With that, Linda and I headed out to find a restaurant. Finding a little secluded place that you would normally have to have a reservation for was perfect for us. Fortunately, catching the restaurant on a night not needing to have a reservation, we got right in, ate a very fine dinner, and drank until we were both close to having a serious buzz. In fact, I believe she had reached that threshold already.

Arriving at the guest house, I gathered her bags and carried them into the room. Coming close to having to carry Linda into the room would have been disastrous considering I was barely able to carry her bags. Flopping her bags down on the floor and watching her fall onto the bed, I closed the door and flopped down on the bed right next to her. Feeling her movement in getting up, I felt so buzzed I didn't even move. I felt her pulling my boots off and then unzipping my flight suit.

As I opened my eyes and lifted my head slightly, all I saw was Linda crawling on the bed next to me with not a stitch of clothing on.

I remember saying to myself, "You look like an angel."

Feeling her slowly laying her body down on me, the warmth and softness of her was unimaginable. Linda didn't weigh anything. She was five feet four and about 108 lbs and possessed one of the most beautiful bodies a guy could ever dream about.

It had been greater than two years since having the pleasure of experiencing the magic of a woman's touch. Looking at me, she was yearning so badly for that sensuous, soft, and caring touch we had provided each other so many years ago. I could not believe we were in a similar situation now as we were then when we had an unbelievably sensuous and intense night of passion.

Years ago, knowing DeLisa was alive, I had surrendered to the fact that she wanted nothing more to do with me. Now it was different. DeLisa had passed. The woman of my dreams was gone. My mind was moving again at the speed of light. Linda was in the picture now. Trying desperately to get DeLisa out of my mind was almost an impossible feat. Linda saw it in my eyes. Her blue eyes were as deep and piercing as DeLisa's green eyes.

She said, "Rob, I have never forgotten that night we were together. I want to care for you like you cared for me that night. You showed me how a person can be so passionate when truly loving them. I care for you like that night we had. You demonstrated how you loved DeLisa that night, and tonight, I am going to show you how I love you. You can pretend I am DeLisa. I don't mind. Just treat me like you would have treated her."

Looking at Linda, I said, "I know you're not DeLisa. I have not been with anyone since her passing. I need you, and I am learning to love you more each day. Just don't give up on me, please."

Looking into those beautiful eyes, I leaned up, and she bent down. Our lips met with the soft passion of a warm oil being gently rubbed in to your entire body.

My hand gently taking her by the neck, I said, "I really need to take a shower. Relax or join me, it's up to you. Regardless, when I'm done, I want to rekindle the passion we had in Galveston. Just you and me, no one else."

I wasn't in the shower for two minutes when I heard the door open and felt her warmth up against my backside. I was not aware of how long we were in the shower, but I remember we ran out of hot water, so we relocated to the bedroom. After that, I remember waking up at about 9:00 a.m. She was sleeping and looked so content. I didn't want to bother her.

When she finally opened those eyes and raised herself up, it was obvious she was pleased she had made the decision to come to Fort Stewart and to be with me.

As I looked at her looking at me, I said, "Thank you for coming and being with me. I did not think a man in this world would have two opportunities in one lifetime to love someone like I loved DeLisa. Linda, I will not make the same mistake I made with her. First, I am in love with you. Second, I do not want to wait in making this a permanent relationship. Will you marry me?"

She looked at me, gazing into my soul, and said, "I would marry you anywhere and anytime. Yes, I will marry you."

She threw the covers off, running at me with that beautiful, naked body, smiling and laughing. Finally wrapping her arms around my neck, she said, "I have dreamed of you asking me that question for about seven years now. Rob, you are my life, and I love you more than you could ever possibly know."

She said, "Have you thought about a date to be married?"

I said, "As soon as you feel comfortable. In the meantime, let's go find somewhere to live. What do you say?"

She definitely was not DeLisa; she was dressed and ready to go out the door in ten minutes and looked like she had been working on those looks for hours. She looked great in jeans, sandals, and a nice blouse. We stopped by the realtor's office, and Linda decided that she wanted to see the two apartments and one of the houses. The house was not in a good location, so we discarded that choice. The two apartments were close to the water, and that was the reason I selected them. I knew she remembered the way she felt with that almost calm warm summer ocean breeze through my sliding glass door in Galveston and that sensuous night we shared. The last apartment we looked at was very similar to that very apartment I was living in down in Galveston. She noticed it too.

As we talked more about us being together, I explained all the training I was going to have to be involved with for the next few months. Linda was good with that as long as I came home for her at night or day whenever I was off work. She began setting up the apartment like we were already married. I had no problem with that; I had already accepted her as my significant other.

It was time for me to start organizing my combat crews, selecting my unit trainers, and addressing any problematic children we might have.

Calling all the flight crew members into operations, I sat the five NVG PICs in the front row. All other warrants, crew chiefs, and medics stood around the room. The most senior warrant officer got the opportunity to choose his copilot first, the second most senior warrant officer did the same, and so on and so on until the five PICs had their choice of the copilots they wanted.

I asked all the remaining crew members except the remaining pilots to take a break outside for five minutes.

After they departed, I looked at all the crews and stated, "Is every crew satisfied with one another's choices? Now be aware, you people are going to spending a lot of time in training with one another, so you're going to need to get along with one another. Respect one another, and know when the PIC makes their decision, that's it. Does everybody understand? Now does anyone want to change?"

Two copilots decided they did not want to be assigned with their two PICs. There were four warrants left of which two were NVG qualified and current. They were happy to replace the two who did not want to fly with those specific PICs.

So we now had five identified combat flight crews and four pilots and three officers. I needed to figure out which of them were going to be my sixth combat crew.

After my meeting with the CW3, he had agreed to change his attitude and to become more involved in supporting the unit's needs. Because of his experience, I offered him the position of being the PIC for the sixth combat crew, if he would get signed off as an NVG PIC within the next thirty days. He told me in no uncertain terms he would be happy to make that happen. I took him under my wing and trained him up, and in less than twenty days, he was a qualified and current NVG PIC.

We had six solid NVG combat crews who were qualified and current. I still had the commander, operations officer, a platoon leader, and two W-1s. I made all of them designated backup crews in the event a member of a crew was unable to fly for whatever reason. The operations officer was an NVG PIC, and I designated one of the warrant officers to be his copilot. Additionally, the commander was not going to be doing much flying as an air mission commander, so I designated myself as the final NVG PIC with the pilots for combat crews.

After all the pilots settled and accepted their roles, I called the crew chiefs/mechanics in. The seven crews were separated in the room, so the crew chiefs could see the personnel makeup of each pilot and copilot. I designated the most experienced crew chief with the least experienced PIC and went down the list with that concept in mind. The selection process worked out well, and our experience was leveled across the entire unit.

Captain Smith and the commander were very pleased with the setup, and we began training operations based on our contingencies.

After flying with two crews per night for six days, I assigned reading assignments to the flight crews that were to be discussed after the three annual evaluations I had to complete. Calling the three members in for their flight evaluations, I briefed them that they were in their windows for their evaluations to be completed. At any time between now and the end of the month, I would call them in to conduct their oral evaluation and schedule their flight portions. In the meantime, their written exam would be tomorrow at 0900 hours. They were all ready to get the evaluations over with.

After the three evaluations were completed, concentrating back on the combat crew PICs, each PIC was demonstrated the techniques of landing in the dust and sand and thus overcoming a brown-out situation. The same techniques could be used in a snow environment, also eliminating the possible white-out situation. After teaching the PICs and signing their training off, the same training was given to the copilots. The crew members were taught how to call out the altitude of the aircraft before it touched down, plus what position relative to the aircraft the dust clouds were at, so the pilots could expect when the brown-out would engulf the aircraft.

All the crews seemed to be able to perform the brown-out task with a proficiency like they had been performing it five hundred times.

Calling the six PICs in my office, I decided to initiate the mentorship program again. A new warrant officer not having anyone to talk to or ask questions to without repercussions, in my opinion, was vital to their success as a young warrant officer. I sat down with them and assigned every warrant who arrived in the unit less than one year ago a mentor. It started working, with positive affects almost immediately.

Giving the commander his first monthly briefing and discussing the current unit's combat readiness, he was not only pleased but was also surprised at the progress that had been made. In discussing the results of the training for our contingency, he was just shaking his head in a satisfactory way. He couldn't believe we had made the amount of progress that we did in one month. He was excited about me scheduling a flight for him to be an observer with one of the combat crew training events under goggles. Though he was a trained pilot, being a commander did not leave much time for him to do a lot of flying. It was my job as the unit instructor to make sure he could do many of the maneuvers required by his pilots.

Deciding to take about three days off and waking up with Linda were equivalent to being in heaven. She was so excited about me having the three days off.

I asked her, "Have you decided when you would like to get married?"

As she leaned on me with her soft warmth, she said, "I think I would like a fall wedding. What about you?"

I said, "It sounds wonderful. The weather should be cooler. The leaves maybe falling, and if you're happy, that makes me happy."

I asked her, "Would you like to take a day drive with me tomorrow?"

She stated she would be really happy with that and asked, "Where are we going?"

I said, "I would like to see what you think of a place in Destin called the Henderson Park Inn for a wedding venue."

She said, "I would love to!"

Looking at me with such a satisfied and yet needy gaze, I couldn't do anything but to pull her down to me on the bed, wrapping her in my arms and holding her tight. Softly kissing her became the button for turning on her passion.

Spending half the day in bed and the other on the apartment docks, she was probably the happiest woman in the world. We went out for dinner that night, and after returning to the apartment, we packed an overnight bag for Destin. Pinging off the walls, her excitement was barely containable, but she persevered. We decided to get an early start, but her excitement was uncontrollable. Her overflowing passion was something you could only dream about.

Finally, at around 2:00 a.m., she fell into a deep and acutely fatigued sleep. Watching her being so content sleeping next to me and thinking how fortunate I have been in knowing two women such as I have had to have been God's will. I do not think any single man could be this lucky.

CHAPTER 13

Here Comes the Sand

Finally dosing off and becoming so comfortable next to Linda's warmth, hearing my phone ring at about 7:00 a.m. startled me to the point of almost experiencing a heart attack. Jumping up, heart racing, and trying to gather my thoughts with my mind in light-speed mode, I suddenly heard a familiar voice on the phone.

"Mr. Lancaster, is that you?"

I wondered why Captain Smith was calling me, knowing I had the day off.

He said, "You need to get dressed and come in ASAP. We may be deploying oversees. Don't bring your go bag yet, we have time to do those things. We are just getting a brief right now."

I said, "Roger that, sir. I'll be there in twenty minutes."

Linda, not accustomed to deployments at all due to being in recruiting, was thinking the worst.

I told her, "This is only a brief right now, and we do not know what's going on. It may just be an exercise, so let's not worry until we know something."

She just hugged and kissed me as I walked out the door.

Looking back at her, I said, "I love you," as I blew her a kiss.

Driving into the airfield and remembering how Captain Smith sounded, there was a feeling developing in my stomach that said to my brain this might be serious. We were going to deploy. Thinking about our contingency, it would most likely be to the Middle East somewhere.

There was a rumor Iraq was invading a country called Kuwait, which nobody even knew where it was. Our commander wanted everyone notified, all their gear checked, and a list of any equipment needed. All the warrant officers showed, and their equipment were checked. The pilots were ready for whatever was going to be thrown at them.

Calling all the warrant officer pilots in a separate room, I said, "Gentlemen, this might just be the real thing. I want to make sure you and your families do not need anything, and if they do, we need to know what those needs are so we can support our people. I gave out Linda's contact number for all the guys' wives to have in the event we were deployed, and they needed something."

I called Linda and asked her to be the wives' representative between the warrant officers' wives and the Army. She jumped all over the chance to contribute. Being in the military before, she knew all the contacts required for certain needs without being given the runaround.

As all plans were in place for the unit and all equipment were ready, we were sent home to be with our loved ones because we discovered our deployment was imminent. It was emphasized: stay close to your phone and have your go bags next to the front door.

Getting all the flight crews together, I told them, "No one knows how they are going to perform in any situation until they are placed in that situation. I want everyone in this room to look at their brethren next to them and promise them they will not let them down. In many cases, we are the only savior our warriors can turn to when they need help. Remember what we trained for and how we trained. Our combat brothers know us as the warrior's savior."

In the upcoming third book of the series *The Warrior's Savior*, *Feeling the Shock and Awe* exposes mind-blowing events of unimaginable magnitudes.

If you have experienced the first two books in the series, *The Woman Who Captured His Heart* and *In the Best of Times and the Worst of Times*, the third book will truly be a shock and awe.

ABOUT THE AUTHOR

From being a high school dropout to an Army medevac helicopter instructor pilot, a director of pilot recruiting for the second and third largest regional airlines in the world, and flying more than one thousand five hundred patient evacuation missions in the military and civilian emergency medical operations, very few have experienced Rob Lancaster's adrenaline-filled existence. He can say not one patient has ever passed away on the medevac aircraft he was flying. From picking up the wounded under fire to transporting car accident victims to medical facilities, his days were loaded with "adrenaline busting missions" that crews had no idea what they were getting into until arriving on those scenes.

Rob, being assigned as a medevac pilot and subsequently falling into the Iran-Contra affair in the mid-eighties, began a life of cloak-and-dagger moments that sent emotions never realizing he had to the brink of his sanity. To this day, looking back at so many events that made him the person he is today, it's difficult to imagine he is still alive.

Exposing his most passionate and his deepest sensitivities in this, his second book of the series *The Warrior's Savior* is truly a breakout milestone for Rob Lancaster. The first book was a tearjerker of happiness but cannot compare to the emotions orchestrated on paper in this, *The Warrior's Savior: In the Best of Times and the Worst of Times.*

Many of the events described in the first two books of *The Warrior's Savior* are based off true events in Rob Lancaster's Life. His life has been a whirlwind of adrenaline-flowing encounters most people only dream about. There are going to be three to five more potential books in the future based off the real events during his life.

Do not let any of them get by you!

Book One of the Series:
The Warrior's Savior in The Woman That Captured His Heart.
Readers can purchase this book on Amazon.

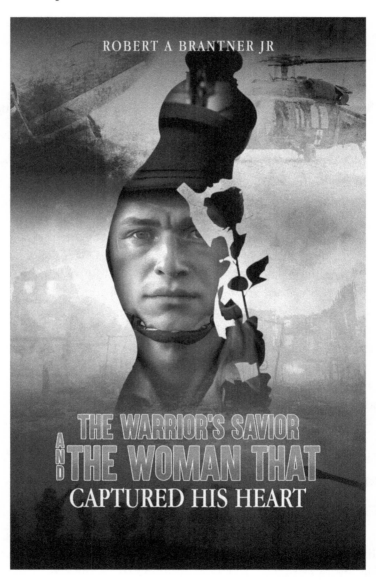

Printed in the USA
CPSIA information can be obtained
at www.ICGtesting.com
LVHW091235210724
786027LV00001B/188